T0149534

The Semi-Lovers

The
Semi-Lovers

Senior Romance is like a Rainbow—Short and Sweet

KENNETH K. SUH

THE SEMI-LOVERS
SENIOR ROMANCE IS LIKE A
RAINBOW—SHORT AND SWEET

iUniverse books may be ordered through booksellers or by contacting:

iUniverse
1663 Liberty Drive
Bloomington, IN 47403
www.iuniverse.com
1-800-Authors (1-800-288-4677)

ISBN: 978-1-5320-5569-0 (sc)
ISBN: 978-1-5320-5570-6 (e)

Library of Congress Control Number: 2018910957

Print information available on the last page.

iUniverse rev. date: 09/21/2018

To my wife, Alice

PROLOGUE

Wives are young men's mistresses, companions for middle age, and old men's nurses.

—Sir Francis Bacon

THE ABOVE QUOTE WAS ONE of many notable remarks in Sir Francis Bacon's 1612 essay "Of Marriage and Single Life." It may hold true even today with the younger generations, but what about with *seniors*, especially widows and widowers? They already were mistresses, companions, and nurses before losing their mates. Do they fall in love and go through it all over again in old age?

All married seniors eventually lose their mates, many of them after bearing demanding nursing responsibilities for a long time. Grief overwhelms them, and they are lonesome. A few of them fall in love and remarry late in life. A few others may become companions or lovers the second time around without getting married in old age—and all while family, friends, and society look askance at them.

CHAPTER 1
Double Rainbows

ONE AFTERNOON DAN WAS DRIVING home from a weekend trip to the mountains. It was mid-October at the peak of Indian summer. The temperature had hovered in the seventies all week.

Suddenly his car radio blared out a severe-weather warning, which was repeated over and over. Dan looked up at the sky and saw ominous thunderclouds behind the foothills. He wanted to get home quickly, but driving was slow going with so many cars returning home from their weekend trips.

Soon storm clouds shut off the sun, engulfed the area, and overtook his car from behind. He had to turn on his headlights. A bolt of lightning ripped the dark sky in front of him and was followed by a gigantic thunderclap. Then a fierce wind whipped at his car, and he heard the rain pounding on his car roof. He soon realized that it was more than just raindrops. He saw tiny hailstones ricocheting off the hood. The hailstorm formed a thick, silvery curtain, and his wipers barely kept the windshield clear.

The hailstorm passed over, but now he had to drive

through torrential rain; it was like driving along a murky river bottom. Dan put on his four-way flashers and drove very slowly. He was concerned about crashing into a car in front of him but just as concerned that the cars behind him would rear-end him. He knew many cars were swimming on that crowded highway.

The unrelenting storm gave no sign of letting up anytime soon. Lightning streaked across the sky like Fourth of July fireworks. Thunder rumbled like an artillery barrage.

Then, after what seemed like an eternity, the storm stopped abruptly. It moved eastward and away as fast as it had arrived. The sky was still dark, but Dan now felt as if he was in a vacuum. Soon bright daylight broke out. Looking through the now-clear windshield, Dan saw no flash flooding in his immediate vicinity.

In his rearview mirror he saw the sun hanging above the dark silhouette of the mountain range. It shined on the back side of the fast-moving, massive, pitch-black storm clouds. Then he saw a bright rainbow—and then another faint one.

A minute later, a weather bulletin on the car radio said a tornado had been sighted in the airport area, which was where the storm system was now located. Dan shivered on thinking that he was under a tornado-bearing storm system, but he did not realize that it could create a stunning double rainbows.

Rainbows

The double rainbows seemed to be an illusion after a grand finale of nature's symphony orchestra—loud thunder, lightning, and a pounding hailstorm. It seemed to be saying, "Sorry, you guys. We're not all that bad. We also have a silver lining."

Dan reflected on his half century in this country and realized he had encountered many storms but had never been rewarded with anything like these beautiful double rainbows. He knew the rainbows would not last forever, so he told himself to enjoy them for as long as possible. He smiled as he asked himself, "What about the pot of gold? Oh no. There should be two pots under these double rainbows."

His eyes followed to the bases of the rainbows. Surprisingly, it seemed to be where his town was located. He found himself rushing. He was not a storm chaser but a rainbow chaser; rather, he was chasing the "pots of gold." It wasn't long before he realized he was not going to find them—not now or anytime soon—as he had never seen any in the past. It was a cruel illusion after another punishing storm.

With the outside symphony having ended, he now heard a trumpet sounding from a classical FM station on his car radio. He soon recognized it as "Solveig's Song." He turned up the volume and continued driving, with the double rainbows still shining in front of him.

"Solveig's Song" had been a favorite since his high school days. He used play it on his cello when he was in med school. In the United States, his cello was his first major investment from his meager intern's salary—it had been three years before he could afford a car. He had played it especially when he was all alone in his dorm on long weekends and holidays.

Since that afternoon, whenever he saw a rainbow, he'd find himself humming Solveig's Song, and whenever he heard Solveig's Song, a rainbow would flash in front of his eyes.

When Dan opened his Facebook account that evening, he saw the ever-present message "People You May Know," which showed a dozen people to whom he might agree to be Facebook friend. He usually ignored the suggestions, but on that night one name stood out. "Lucy Kim Yi. You have three mutual friends." Her name sounded familiar. He kept repeating her name but couldn't place her.

Yi was another Romanized version of Lee, like Rhee, Ri, Li, and Yee. Yi and Kim were very common Korean surnames, much like Smith in America. So Dan assumed that Kim was her maiden surname and Yi was her married name. That didn't help him much, as this Lucy could be one of several million Kims or Lees in the States. Then he realized that *Lucy* was not a commonly used first name among Korean Americans, and his heart suddenly fluttered at a thought that this Lucy Kim Yi could be his friend from almost a half century earlier.

When he was in Chicago, Dan had a half-dozen homesick Korean friends doing graduate studies, both medical and nonmedical. Lucy Kim was one of them. Dan had dated her for three years, but had to part ways, and he had not seen or heard from her since.

Although he'd had his Facebook account for some time, he used it only occasionally, mostly to see what was going on with his family, especially his grandchildren. Long neglected, his Facebook page was now overrun with many second-, third-, and even fourth-generation friends—friends of friends, and friends of friends of other friends. Some were from the far side of the world, and some were even his old enemies' friends—his competitors in practice. He had long ago concluded that Facebook itself was the aggressive "friendship promoter" more for its own benefit.

But Dan now wanted to know who his mutual friends were with Lucy Kim Yi. Among the three, only one was familiar—Helen Choy. Dan recognized her immediately, as she was Dan's med school classmate's wife. Dan had met Philip and Helen a year earlier at the fiftieth reunion of his med school in Seoul, Korea. Then he remembered Helen saying she was from the nursing college of his university and had graduated in the same year as he and Philip had, and their fiftieth reunion was the following week.

Dan became more curious, as if he had found a bottle washed ashore with a message inside. After few more prompts, he was on Lucy's personal Facebook page. There, Dan saw her profile picture and realized she was a complete stranger. She had glasses, gray hair, a nice smile, and a dignified, elderly Asian countenance, but she didn't have any distinguishing feature.

He discovered her given name in Korean was Young-Ja. *Young-Ja?* Again, it was a very common name in Korea, much like Mary in the States. Her bio indicated she was a graduate of a high school in Seoul, but she hadn't specified the school's name. It meant she was from Seoul, but that did not help much. Then Dan saw that Lucy had studied at the College of Nursing at his university and had worked at a university hospital in Chicago.

His heart almost stopped as he realized that Lucy Kim

Yi was directly on the path to his painful and tumultuous past, and the probability of this Lucy Kim Yi being his old sweetheart was high. Yet he told himself, *It's still possible that one or two others with that common name and common background might be around.*

So he pored over her picture, looking for any clues to jog old memories. While few landmarks like the Loop and O'Hare Airport flashed through his mind, he had no idea how Lucy looked when young, although obviously he was looking at her recent Facebook profile picture.

Younger Lucy's image was completely blurred, and Dan could remember only that she'd been a good-looking young lady, headstrong and with a sharp tongue. She was then a blossoming twenty-eight-year-old, while he was an ancient bachelor at thirty.

Dan spent another half hour studying her Facebook page and her picture. He wished he had kept some of her old pictures, but he had disposed of everything just before getting engaged.

He wondered if he could ask for old pictures from other old friends, but they were scattered around the world, and he'd had no contact with any of them for decades.

After another hour of studying her picture, he thought he could see *some resemblance* to the younger Lucy in her Facebook picture—the general countenance, the smile, the eyebrows and kind eyes, slightly magnified by her eyeglasses...all pointed to this lady as his old sweetheart.

Dan wondered how Lucy's voice sounded now and wished he could hear her voice, especially her giggling. Dan had his own pet theory that everyone had a unique giggling pattern, not only in sound but also in body motion.

Dan looked at her picture again and thought it had to be her best—the kind of picture an elderly lady would post on Facebook, possibly even taken as far back as five years. Dan thought that five years earlier, he had been in much better shape than now. Dan was sure Lucy would be shocked and disappointed if she saw him now, a wizened old man.

Dan had health problems. He had a near-fatal heart attack a year earlier. They also found a large ascending aortic aneurysm—a ballooning of the artery—and also moderate aortic stenosis, which was a narrowing of a heart valve. In addition, he had severe back pain and a few other medical problems, as well as a long list of powerful medications he had to take every day.

He posted no profile picture on Facebook. Except for his name and that he was a fellow of the American College of Physicians (FACP), a medical honor society, his Facebook profile was bare; it even omitted other basic information, such as high school, college, or memberships to any organizations.

The pictures he occasionally posted were all group shots, especially of him with his grandchildren, and taken at a distance far enough to reveal no wrinkles. He deleted any of his pictures others posted if his features were too detailed. He had no one to impress. Rather he did not want to give a bad impression to anyone.

The next day Dan became more curious about Lucy, so he went back to her Facebook page and studied it from top to bottom. It was also littered with her friends' pictures and stories, but Dan noticed one thing unique—a photo of a cherubic young boy with the Coliseum in the background and a comment thanking Lucy for his trip.

Suddenly Dan felt guilty, as if he was a Peeping Tom caught in act. He felt he had no business prying into a stranger's private life, whether Lucy Kim's or someone else's. So he closed her Facebook page immediately. Dan also decided there was no reason to revive their relationship after a half century of separate lives, although there was nothing to prohibit their becoming friends, especially on Facebook.

He finally concluded that Facebook was pushing the friendship, not Lucy, and even if they both wanted to be friends, Facebook was not the right forum. It provided no privacy; it was now a wide-open public arena, just like bulletin boards in the post office and supermarket in olden days; and his children, grandchildren, and other friends could see the bizarre melodrama between two seniors.

Over the next few weeks, Dan found himself thinking about Lucy Kim quite often, even though he tried not to. He wondered why he had so hastily closed the door to Lucy Kim when, a half century earlier, they had been great friends and had promised to be friends forever.

He knew he was a train wreck beyond repair. He was falling apart physically, while Lucy still looked so good. He knew there was no cure for his physical deterioration, not even with multiple plastic surgeries and massive Botox injections.

Eventually, he concluded that the fear of rejection was the main reason why he was so afraid of rekindling their friendship. He didn't want to face the inevitable humiliation of being rebuffed and suffering through the remaining few years. So he said to himself, "Don't do anything stupid. Just fade away when your time comes."

Dan thought about their mutual friend Helen and her husband, Philip. The Choys had been in Chicago for a long time. They had come to see him twice in northern Ohio, and Dan and his wife, Linda, had visited them once. He now was able to connect the dots. Most likely Lucy and Helen were nursing college alumnae and could have been friends in Chicago.

Another few weeks passed. Whenever Dan opened up Facebook, he saw many strangers being suggested as friends. He would delete them, but then some of them would reappear, but to his great disappointment, Lucy's name never reappeared, once her name had been deleted.

Dan was sorry he'd deleted Lucy's name so impulsively, when it was only a suggestion to become Facebook friends. He wasn't quite sure how the "friends" thing worked on Facebook, so at times he wondered if Lucy herself had made the request, rather than the ever-pushy Facebook, and he felt ill for deleting her name prematurely before things were clear.

He had vowed to see everyone he wanted to see before he died, and he was hoping to go to Korea one last time to say goodbye to his parents' tombs and see his remaining siblings and few childhood friends, even though he had seen them only a year earlier.

Likewise, he concluded that if Lucy was dying to see him, he would see her so that she could close a nostalgic chapter. He was afraid Lucy might have some grave medical issues and wanted to see him before too late, and that made him feel worse.

Just after the New Year's Day when he logged on to his Facebook account, he again saw the ever-present prompt "People You May Know." While perusing them one by one, he could not believe his eyes—Lucy Kim Yi. He was sure Facebook was pushing, but this time it did not matter. He promptly agreed to be her friend—with a great sigh of relief.

Now he decided to contact his old classmate Philip. He was out golfing when Dan called, but when Philip returned the call, they had a nice chat. Philip was pleasantly surprised that Dan was trying to be a Facebook friend with Lucy. Philip knew Lucy Kim very well. He confirmed to Dan that she was his wife Helen's classmate, and they had been friends in Chicago for three decades.

"Funny that you should mention Lucy," Philip said. "We were surprised when she asked, 'Which one is Dan Ahn?', while we were showing her some of our reunion pictures. Her husband was one year ahead of us in medical school. He passed away few years ago. You might remember him—Charles Yi."

It was another surprise to Dan because he'd known Charles Yi very well. He had been Dan's resident physician when Dan was an intern at a university hospital in Seoul.

Later, Philip sent him Lucy's email address and phone number.

Dan emailed Lucy the same day.

Hi, Lucy,

I am Dan Ahn. Today I talked to Philip Choy of San Diego, our mutual friend. I met Choys last year in Seoul at the fiftieth reunion. He gave me your email address and phone number as well. Two months ago I saw your name suggested as a Facebook friend but I couldn't tell if it was you or the Facebook making the suggestion, but when I saw it again today, I promptly agreed on. If it wasn't you, please forgive me. Also, please forgive me for writing this in email. I didn't want to use Facebook for personal matters.

I guessed all along that you were happily married, but didn't know Dr. Charlie Yi was the lucky guy. I'm very sorry that he passed away. He was very nice to me when I was an intern under him. Hope to talk to you and even meet with you.

Take good care of yourself, and happy New Year.

Dan

Dan also included his phone numbers and address in the email.

After that, he checked his email and Facebook every day, but two weeks passed without any news from Lucy. Then one evening, she called. He didn't answer it because the phone number on the caller ID was unfamiliar; he let it go to voice mail. Curious, he looked at the phone number again and found it was from a Chicago suburb. His heart was pounding as he listened to the voice mail recording.

"Hi, Dan. This is Lucy Kim in Chicago, your old friend..."

After just those few words, Dan remembered the sound of her voice. In his excitement, he almost erased the recording. When recovered, he played the rest of it.

"Philip and Helen said you're doing well after your heart attack, but I am just nosy and wanted to talk to you. Take care, and have a great day."

He had to take several deep breaths to calm down. He played the recording repeatedly. Her voice had been so ingrained in his brain that he knew right away it was Lucy's, his old sweetheart, and he wondered how he could have forgotten her voice. He had exactly the same feeling as when he heard his mother's voice for the first time in ten years at the Los Angeles Airport. "You never forget your mom's voice, even ten or twenty years later," Dan had said then.

He checked the time. It was seven in the evening in Denver but eight o'clock in Chicago—not too late for a *social call*—so he called Lucy. She answered on the first ring.

"Hello, is it Lucy Kim?"

"Yes. It must be Dr. Snail."

"Beg your pardon?"

"We used to call you Dr. Snail because you were so slow. Don't you remember?"

"Yes, I do, my dear Miss Swiss Cheese."

"Swiss Cheese?"

"Yes, we used to call you Swiss Cheese because you were a stubborn ole miss. You don't remember that? That guy, Dr. Chu, said all the old maidens, especially good-looking ones, had unique brain lesions with multiple cavities, like Swiss cheese. He was a pathology fellow at Cook County Hospital."

"Yes, now I remember."

It was clear that he was talking to Lucy, his old sweetheart.

"It really took you a long time to catch up with me, Dr. Snail," Lucy continued.

"Yes, forty-five years to be exact. How are you doing, Lucy? How is your health? You looked great in your Facebook picture." Health was the most important matter to seniors their age.

"I'm doing all right with some hip pains. How about you, Dan? I didn't see you in any of your pictures on Facebook."

"I'm a wizened old man, so I can't show my face."

As they talked, each of them asked "Remember that?" umpteen times and strained their ears—more to get reacquainted with each other's voice than for the topics of conversation, although Dan was sure they covered everything, even the windy Chicago weather.

After almost an hour, as they were winding down, Lucy asked, "Can you send me some recent pictures?"

"Oh, you want to see how ugly I am? Yes, I will, but only if you reciprocate."

"I'll do that, Dan."

After a pause, Dan said, "Hey Lucy, please be open-minded."

"What do you mean, Dan?" Lucy seemed surprised.

"When you see me for the first time in forty-five

years, even in pictures, you might be disappointed over the tremendous metamorphosis."

"Metamorphosis?"

"Yes, I've turned to an ugly monster. Some people get so shocked they wish they'd never seen me in person or even in pictures. I'm far better in memories than the actual guy."

"Huh. We are no longer spring chickens. We're old, sluggish, senile hens and roosters, but as we exchange more pictures, the shock will diminish," said Lucy, trying to comfort Dan. "Okay, Dan? The fear of rejection is natural at our age. It's mutual, especially after forty-five years. We could use FaceTime and Skype when we both build up our self-esteem and aren't so shy with each other."

"Yes, Lucy." Then Dan asked, "Lucy, would you please do me just one more favor?"

"Like what, Dan?"

"Could you possibly send me some old pictures of yourself when we were in Chicago?"

"What's that for?"

"I've spent last two months trying to figure out how you might have looked in Chicago. I have to get reconnected to my young Juliet first before we go any further."

"What if there isn't any?"

"Aha! Then we're totally doomed."

"Ha! It's okay, Dr. Snail. That's not the end of the world."

CHAPTER 2
San Francisco Airport

Lucy and Dan kept in touch. Pictures and email crossed half the continent, east and west. Phone calls and texts flew over the time zones. They also Googled to learn more about each other and spouses.

Dan wondered how people wrote love letters in this era of cell phones, texting, email, FaceTime, and Skype. Perhaps they didn't but interacted in real time with the omnipresent and omnipotent smartphones, unlike the olden days, when letters took a long time to go back and forth, even with the air mail.

Although they agreed on a Facebook friendship, it was difficult to know how far they were going. Dan was afraid of falling in love. He knew they both were vulnerable now that they were lonesome after being widowed for three years and especially because they had been in love before. On the other hand, Dan still was afraid of being rebuffed by his former sweetheart. It would be catastrophic for him.

Dan heard numerous anecdotes of disappointments when former sweethearts met for the first time in many decades. So he did not want a rejection of any kind from

Lucy and wanted to be careful of doing anything more than a Facebook friendship.

One day in mid-January, Lucy surprised Dan when she said, "I am going to visit Korea."

"Is someone ill?"

"No. I just want to see my family."

"When are you going?"

"January 30."

"Aha," Dan said.

"Aha, what?"

"I have to go to Korea around that time also, for a wedding."

"Wedding?" Lucy was surprised.

"My niece is getting married. She's my youngest sister's youngest daughter and is thirty-three years old."

After a pause Dan asked, "Are you going alone?"

"Yes, all alone."

"Directly from Chicago to Seoul?"

"There's a layover in San Francisco."

"Aha!"

"Aha, again? What's that supposed to mean this time?"

"Do you think I can tag along with you to Seoul?" Dan asked, without answering her question.

Lucy was stunned. "Beg your pardon?" When Dan did not respond, Lucy asked him again, "What did you say just now?"

After a pause Dan said calmly, "I want to go to Seoul with you, riding in same airplane, if possible."

Lucy could not believe what Dan was saying.

"What's that for?"

"That could be the quickest way to meet with you and the best way to get reacquainted."

"Um... uh..." Lucy was bewildered, but Dan was excited.

"There isn't a direct flight to Seoul from Denver, so I have to go to San Francisco, Los Angeles, Seattle, or even Chicago or Dallas to get a connection," he explained.

"What airline do you fly?"

Still in shock, Lucy barely finished saying "United," when Dan cried, "Aha!"

Lucy was more baffled now. "Aha, *again*?"

But Dan was excited. "Then with a modicum of luck, I could join you in San Francisco and fly together. Did you buy your tickets already?"

"Yes, Dan."

"If you don't mind my sitting next to you, I'd like to fly with you. Could you let me know the flight and seat numbers?"

Lucy could not think clearly. After a long pause, Lucy said, "That sounds like an interesting proposition. Let me think about it, Dan. I'll let you know soon."

Dan felt like he'd been doused with ice water. He was deeply disappointed at her cool reception to his idea, although he knew it was quixotic.

Dan waited anxiously for Lucy's response, and he clung to the hope that she would not decline. After one full week, he started to worry about her rejection, but on the other hand, he also worried that she might accept his audacious proposal—there was a saying that at times people did not know what to do when a dream came true.

On the eighth day, she emailed her flight information

unceremoniously, without fanfare, but also without the seat number. Dan was excited, so he called her immediately to thank her for her permission and also to ask for her seat number. She did not remember the seat number right then but promised to text it.

As soon as he had her seat information, Dan rushed to the airline website and looked into the seat availability. Lucy's flight was almost full. Her seat was an aisle seat, but the middle seat was still available. He had to secure that seat. It seemed like a life-or-death exigency. Otherwise, flying in the same airplane but sitting apart from Lucy in layer after layers of passengers, would cause more angst than going to hell. After a flurry of action, he was able to secure the ticket, sitting next to Lucy.

Only then did he buy a ticket from Denver to San Francisco. He didn't care how long the layover was in San Francisco, but it was only five hours. Then he bought his return ticket for ten days later, knowing that Lucy was staying in Korea another ten days.

Later that night, he called Lucy. "Thanks again letting me fly with you, but I have a couple questions."

"Like what?" She sounded curious.

"You know flying to Korea takes almost one full day. Don't you want to fly first class?"

Lucy sighed. "Oh, Dan, I can't afford it."

Dan persisted. "How about a little upgrade to business class?"

"I don't think so. I'll fly the economy, just like the olden days. How about you? If you want to get an upgrade, you just go ahead."

"No way, Lucy. I want to fly with you, side by side. The first-class and business-class seats are far apart."

Lucy complained, "You're now an obnoxious bourgeoisie who despises proletariat."

Dan moaned. "Please don't talk like a trigger-happy Communist political cadre. I've been a proletariat forever. We all worked hard with our bare hands—blood and sweat—in the American gulag. I have one more question. Why do you fly United? Why not Korean Air or Asiana?"

"You're questioning my patriotism? I'm now an impoverished American tourist compared to those nouveau riche Koreans. Korean airlines are good for all the Korean meals, but I have a frequent flyer account with United. Incidentally, that flight is the cheapest around that time."

"I also have a frequent flyer account with United and enough points to upgrade both of us to business class."

As the travel date approached, Dan worried that finding Lucy in the vast San Francisco airport would be like finding a needle in haystack, although they had exchanged their pictures through email and texts. To make things easier, Dan suggested they keep their phones on and pay special attention to the text messages.

That was when Lucy said, "Hey, Dan, why don't I wear a red scarf and red hat? It will be better than carrying a big placard with your name—Dr. Snail—on it."

"Just like color tags on our bags. I'll wear a red baseball cap, but we can still lose our precious cargos."

Lucy was calm: "We can use phones as well."

The day before they were going to meet, Dan emailed Lucy.

> As we talked before, when we meet for the first time in forty-five years, you might be shocked at how much I have changed. If I disappoint you one way or another, please feel free to kick me out. A gorilla sitting next to you all the way to Seoul could be more than a pain in the rear. I am sending this idea via email to give you a quiet time to think about it, rather than over the phone.

A few hours later, Lucy sent a return email.

> Yes, sir, I understand. I request the same to you too.

Later, they talked over the phone, and sent selfies with red hats.

Dan arrived at the San Francisco airport first and looked at Lucy's arrival schedule. He was three hours ahead of her. They had agreed to meet near the departure gate inside the international terminal. The anticipation of meeting his long-ago sweetheart was like sitting on needles, but there also was the fear of rejection and humiliation.

Soon after her arrival time, Dan texted: "I'm near the gate with a red hat."

Lucy texted back: "Okay, see you soon."

Sometime later, Dan saw an Asian lady rushing down the hallway wearing a red hat, red scarf, and glasses. She had to be Lucy. Dan stood up and waved at her. She recognized him immediately and smiled.

It was their first meeting in forty-five years. Holding hands, they bowed to each other—a full ninety degrees—in slow motion. When they were young, that had been their Korean custom when greeting a friend of the opposite gender. Only then did they hug each other, and they stayed that way for a long time, without saying a word. Dan saw tears trickling down Lucy's face, just like when they'd bid farewell in the busy Chicago Loop, almost a half century earlier.

A moment later, Dan tickled Lucy, making her giggle.

Startled, Lucy protested, "Why did you do that, Dan?"

"I wanted to verify that you're my Juliet, not a phantom."

Even before Dan finished talking, Lucy tickled him. "Now I know for sure that you're my Romeo, not an imposter." She smiled wistfully. "We used to tickle a lot in the olden days."

Then they hugged again—a long embrace—and Dan asked, "Are you hungry, my sweetheart?"

"Glad to hear that 'sweetheart' from you again, Dan. I'm not hungry, but I am thirsty, darling," Lucy said, smiling.

"We have two hours to kill. Would you like to go to that Japanese place? It looks popular; it's full of Asians."

"Okay," said Lucy, and she smiled again.

They sat across the table from each other, their gazes locked. They sent out powerful beams, appraising and scrutinizing each other. When Lucy put her hands on the table, Dan grabbed them immediately, and soon their fingers were interlocked. Dan felt sparks flying between their hands, and soon his heart pounded hard, as if Lucy had jump-started his broken heart with her supercharged energy.

Meeting an old sweetheart after all those years was an earth-shattering event. Having seen pictures and having heard her voice over the phone, the shock was much less than it might have been, Dan thought. Dan could not believe that Lucy was sitting in front of him, as if she had come back from a long journey behind the dark side of the moon. He soon realized that he was with Lucy—a 3-D real person in real time—firmly connected by her two warm hands and her two piercing brown eyes.

As if using microscope, Dan scanned every nano-square inch of her face and meticulously studied her expressions, body language, dress, and scent. He could not move his eyes. His brain had to reorient, readjust, and glue back millions of shattered dreams and fantasies. Dan knew Lucy was doing the same with the massive task of reassessing and modifying her memories of him.

Dan thought Lucy, sitting in front of him, looked just like her Facebook profile picture, and he saw many of younger Lucy's vestiges on her present grandmotherly visage. She was elegant and still svelte.

They ordered their meals and ate the seafood udon in complete silence, even without making slurping sounds. Chopsticks moved slowly, and they could not take their eyes off each other.

Finally, Dan said, "Lucy, you look great. You don't look seventy-three years old. You look ten years younger."

"Oh my. You're still so sweet."

It was nice to hear her delicate voice, face-to-face.

"You're not looking so bad yourself, Dan—only a few grays. Considering your recent heart attack and hard labor in the American gulag, you look much better than I was imagining. How are you feeling?" Lucy was genuinely concerned.

"Thanks, I feel fair. How about you, Lucy?"

"I have arthritis, high blood pressure, and high cholesterol—common problems among seniors. Also migraine headaches."

"Nothing major?"

"No, but I feel my age, and it sucks."

To seniors of their age, nothing was more important than health, and Dan was greatly relieved that Lucy was in good health.

"So you married Dr. Charles Yi. It's a small world, Lucy. As I said before, he was my resident physician for three months."

"It *is* a small world, as you said. I met him right after you deserted me. He was just like you. Sometimes I couldn't tell if I was with him or you. So I fell in love with him right away. Perhaps it was a rebound, after being jilted."

"Perhaps. Life has a way of working out for the best..."

"No sense in talking about our bygone days. We promised to stay friends and keep in touch, but it wasn't until last year that Philip and Helen told me that you almost died of a heart attack. I prayed for you and decided to check on you."

"Thanks lot, Lucy." Dan felt a lump in his throat, and tears clouded his vision.

They were quiet for a long time before Lucy asked, "Your wife was a librarian?"

Surprised, Dan asked, "Yes. Helen told you?"

"Who else, Dan? Helen and I were college classmates. We grew older together in Chicago." Then she said, "Hey, Dan. I'm glad that you made it all right."

"Thanks again, Lucy. I needed four stents, but my cardiologist could put in only three." Dan almost choked again, and he put his head down.

"But it looks like you are doing well."

Dan struggled to calm his emotions. "Yes, but I have a few other unexpected problems."

At that moment they were interrupted as the waitress brought their check.

They had another hour to kill, so they moved to the lounge area and sat side by side. Dan asked to see Charlie's picture. After looking at it for some time, Dan said, "I can still see Charlie's old self, even almost fifty years later. Was the picture taken after his retirement?"

"Yes, he got sick only two years into his retirement."

At that moment, a waiter brought their beers, so Dan said, "May this be the first of many to come."

Dan said he was sidetracked earlier; he meant to tell her that he had other medical problems. "I have a big aortic aneurysm and moderate aortic stenosis, but I did not tell the Choys."

"Aneurysm? Abdominal?"

"No, Lucy. It is in ascending aorta."

"Oh my."

Lucy knew it was next to the heart, less common than the abdominal aneurysm and more difficult to repair. It could rupture, causing sudden death.

"How big is it, Dan?"

"It's big—4.6 centimeters. The critical size for a spontaneous rupture is 5.0."

Lucy stopped him. "Dan. Explain it in plain English to a full-time grandma, not to a retired nursing professor," she complained.

Dan suspected she didn't want to hear the bad news. He told her what his doctors had said. "It normally grows one millimeter per year, but in some people, it grows faster. So I have to recheck with an echocardiogram or CT scan every six months and will need surgery when it reaches five centimeters."

When she was quiet, Dan said, "I have four years until the surgery."

"Four years only?" Lucy said, her heart broken.

Dan nodded.

"What about the aortic stenosis?" She was referring to the narrowing of a heart valve. "It's moderate as of now, but my surgeon thinks it will get worse first, and when he fixes it, he'd repair the aneurysm at the same time."

A few minutes later, Lucy said, "Initially, it was shocking, and I thought it was bad, but now I don't think so. You'll be seventy-nine by the time you need the aneurysm repaired. At least you'll have solid four years guaranteed, while most of us don't know what's lurking, let alone how soon it will end us. So you should enjoy each and every day as if it's your last."

"Thank you, Lucy."

He felt his heart warming again. He was sure she was trying to cheer him up.

They were silent for a long time. After another sip of beer, Lucy said, "How do you feel about it?"

"It's all my own fault. I've neglected my own health."

"Mea culpa is for the past. I am asking you about the future."

"I accept my fate—that it is there and that it may rupture at any time. So I've been living on a short leash, getting it extended every six months."

"How do your children feel about it?"

"They know their payday is coming a little bit sooner."

"Payday?"

"Yes, my estate distribution when I die, although not that big."

Lucy was not amused "Don't be so morbid, Dan. Do you have a DNR order?"

"Yes. Also, they will not artificially feed me. How about you, Lucy?"

"Same," she said.

Lucy took another sip. "What are you going to do about it?"

He didn't answer right away. "I'll have to take an elective surgery at five and hope to survive the surgery, rather than after the rupture. The mortality rate is very high, even if it ruptures in a hospital setting, they said. At times, I feel like forgetting the whole thing altogether, considering my age and the fact that I have had a good life. But I still have four years to think about it."

"What are the odds if you take an elective surgery?" Lucy was persistent.

"My surgeon said 2 percent of patients die. Considering my age, he said chance of my dying is 3 per cent.""

"That means 97 percent will survive. That's not bad. Medical science and medical devices have improved tremendously, and you're relatively healthy."

Soon Dan said, "I realize everything is in God's hands."

"Do you go to church?" Lucy asked.

When they were young, many Koreans did not have any religious affiliations because they were forced into Confucianism in the fourteenth century when Buddhism was kicked out of the population centers, and it was only after the Korean War of 1950–1953, when Christianity became popular.

"I just started to go," said Dan, smiling.

"Why? Getting religion in later years?"

"Of course. It's up to the Lord, but..." He shrugged.

Lucy was curious and prodded him to continue. "You know that in America no one can be buried without a minister or priest. They are the true gatekeepers. I can't see Saint Peter until after my funeral. That's the real reason why I started to go to church."

"As a funeral arrangement?"

"Yes, dear."

"Huh." She was in deep thought for several minutes but then said, "That's quite a contrast from when you were young. I know you used to be an avid Christmas Christian."

"Yes, I couldn't miss Christmas festivities—all the parties, choirs, and carols. So I went to church but only at Christmas time."

After another long pause, Lucy smiled broadly and said, "I have a perfect solution for you." Dan looked at her expectantly, and Lucy said, "I agree with you that a former Christmas Christian deserves a decent Christian burial with a proper Christian service. So if you can manage to die on or around Christmas—right in the church, if possible—you could get everything in one clean package."

With that, Lucy erupted into a guffaw. Her laughter was so infectious, first it made Dan smile, and then join in her guffaw, both of them clapping their hands.

The atmosphere was instantly lighter, even if her joke was macabre. It was the first time Dan had seen Lucy laugh in forty-five years. In retrospect, Dan remembered Lucy laughing hard in self-delight whenever she had very funny or cynical ideas, like all the geniuses did. Dan had never laughed as much with anyone as he did with Lucy. She still was a fun person.

Lucy was pensive but then asked, "Do you have any regrets, Dan?"

"I used to have millions but none now."

"How did you manage that?"

"Right after my heart attack, I buried them all, just one step ahead of me, and I have a clean slate---carpe diem."

"Oh, the 'seize the day' thing? Make hay while the

sun shines? Don't you have a special wish to see some people, visit certain places, eat certain food, or smoke the last cigarette... or pot?"

"Not really, Lucy. I've done those things already, but I really wish I could win a jackpot because I am not leaving much to my grandkids. Another wish is that I'll finish my manuscript before my aneurysm pops."

"Good luck with the jackpot, Dan. The kids will enjoy sports cars, but what's the story about the manuscript? Are you writing a book?"

Dan nodded, and Lucy asked, "What about?"

"I'll tell you everything some other time, but it's a short love story, and I've been working on it forever."

"Oh my God. I never knew that a man of so few words and also a man known for having kaleidoscopic brain could write a novel."

"Gee! Thanks for such a high compliment. My family and friends felt same when I published my first book, which they ignored completely. It was the same with my second book. My third likely will get the same reaction, but I don't care."

"Oh my! This is your third? It could be a blockbuster this time—your swan song." Lucy was quiet for a while and then asked, "Can I read your books?"

Dan grinned, "I happen to have several copies in my big suitcase and would be happy to give them to you in Seoul. And in case of a mishap, you also can find them easily through e-book outlets."

Chapter 3
Plane Talks

Soon boarding started. It was a full flight, and it took some time for them to get seated. Dan squeezed into the middle seat first. When Lucy settled into her aisle seat, Dan asked, "Do I get promoted to the business class, Lucy?"

She didn't understand him right away but then said, "Oh no, Dan. You have a detention order to that teensy middle seat. You're stuck here for the entire journey and have to serve me as your special Facebook friend."

"Are you sure?" Dan clearly was happy. When Lucy nodded, he asked, "With all the troubles I have?" She nodded again. "I am honored. I'm going to serve you as my goddess." After a long pause, Dan said, "How about both of us moving to business class? It won't cost us a penny if we use my points."

"No, Dan. We are stuck together right here in this journey." A few minutes later, Lucy whispered, "Do you want to exchange seats, Dan? I know you old boys have to use restroom quite often."

"Thanks, but I'll wake you up whenever it's needed... to prevent blood clots in your legs."

Once airborne, they both purchased Wi-Fi and accessed their laptops. Lucy showed Dan her family pictures, including all three children and seven grandkids. Her son was a doctor, and her two girls were CPAs. The grandkids were beautiful. One boy was an early teen.

"Was it this boy who went to Europe last year?" Dan asked.

Lucy was surprised. "Yes, how did you know?"

"Facebook. I saw him thanking you."

"Yes, that's him. He goes to high school next year."

Dan also showed Lucy his family pictures on his laptop. At mealtime, Dan ordered red wine for each of them so they could toast their trip together.

Later they talked about their spouses. It was a painful subject, but they had to go over it at least once. Lucy was in tears. Dan held her hand while she gave him a brief summary.

Charlie had developed back pain and stomachaches, but he refused to see a specialist, in spite of Lucy's urging, until he became jaundiced. After just few tests they found he had pancreatic cancer, and it was inoperable. He had a simple bypass surgery to drain the bile from the gallbladder to the intestine, and he received radiation therapy and then chemotherapy, but he didn't do well. Hospice was called in soon afterward. Lucy kept him at home and took care of him over the next five months.

"I had professional help, but it was tough to see him wither. Life was hectic, but now, after three years, things have settled down. The kids and grandkids have been great."

Dan was overwhelmed. "Still, one never gets over it

completely. Were you physically well enough to give a good nursing?"

"No, my hips were bad, which made me feel guilty."

"You were shielded from the war and hunger in your childhood and pampered throughout your adolescence, college years, and adult life. Charlie's dying in your arms in your senior years could have been the worst time in your whole life."

"No, it was my second worst time, Dan. The first was when you deserted me. You two were doubles, and I suffered fatal blows from you both."

"Oh my," Dan moaned.

Dan said his wife, Linda, had died of a stroke around the same time that Charlie died.

"Did she linger for a long time, like Charlie?" Lucy asked.

"Yes. I kept her at home for six months, but she ended up in a nursing home for three months in a semicoma, debilitated. Although I had excellent professional help, it was hard for me to take care of her because of my back pain and limping, but..."

"But what?"

"Her personality changed about a year before the stroke," Dan explained. "She gambled a lot, which she hadn't done previously. She became increasingly upset, irritating everyone, especially family members. Later, she became a terrible patient—onerous, angry, very demanding, and cruel to her caregivers. Basically, she was angry at the world and angrier at anyone healthier than she was."

"Did you say gambling? What kind?"

"Poker."

"Linda probably had a brain aneurysm. I've seen several people's personalities change near the rupture," Lucy said, holding Dan's hands.

"I'll bet Charlie was nice to you and all the caregivers."

"Yes, to the end."

"God bless him."

Lucy reflected on what they'd discussed. "Still, our spouses were physically ill, unlike those suffering from Alzheimer's. I have quite a few friends who went through the hell."

"I agree. Alzheimer's is a curse, especially when one starts to wander."

Dan wanted to cheer Lucy up. Still holding her hand, he said, "I have many nice memories of Charlie also. Do you want to hear some of them?" When she nodded, Dan said, "We did quite a few extracurricular activities together. I'll give you just one episode today and the rest in installments."

"You're trying to blackmail me. You know I'm a sugar grandma."

"Of course, but I'm a sugar grandpa. We're after each other for money, are we not? Anyway, Charlie and I did quite few things together."

"Such as?" Then she screamed, "Oh my God. Don't tell me that you guys went to geisha houses and lost your virginity together." Lucy was now wide-awake.

"Oh no. Not that, but we did drink a lot. We were drinking buddies."

Lucy was incredulous. "He got drunk? With geishas?"

"Yes, but more often it was just us, when we got back to the dorm after leaving the geishas."

"Oh my. This is first time I've ever heard him drinking. He was a devout Christian. Korean Christians don't drink, or smoke, as you know," Lucy said, shaking her head.

"It was the best time in my whole life."

"Being drunk?"

"Yes. Mostly binge drinking and passing out."

"Oh my."

"As I said, I have more stories, but I think this is enough for today."

"You bastard blackmailer."

Lucy settled back in her seat and squeezed Dan's hand. "You miss Linda very much, don't you, Dan."

"Yes, it's been like a gaping hole."

"Can I see her picture again?"

He showed her a picture on his cell phone and said, "She was very much like you."

"She was better looking than I. She must have been so pretty when she was young."

"Linda talked and acted just like you. It was almost as if you had come back into my life."

"I sent her to you, Dan. I felt the same with Charlie—as I said, he was a dead ringer for you."

"I sent Charlie to you too."

"Aha!"

"Aha, what, Lucy?"

"I now know that they were the ones who put us together."

"Do you think so?"

"Yes, Dan."

Dan thought about it and then said, "Linda was a control freak, just like you."

"Domineering? Like Xanthippe?"

"Yes. That's the reason why I became a Socrates."

"That's why you're writing too?"

"Yes. She was also a spoiled, obnoxious doctor's wife, Lucy."

"I'm one of them too, but people get jealous over doctors' wives, just in case you didn't know."

"Lucy, you were a professor with encyclopedic knowledge, right? What was the real Xanthippe like in her old age? How did she treat Socrates in later years? Did she ever get mellow, or did she continue to abuse the holy man?"

Lucy shrugged. "Beats me."

"Linda was sickly. Besides three pregnancies, she had many surgeries---her ovaries, uterus, appendix, one middle ear surgery in her fifties. Then she had two knee surgeries, two shoulder operations, and a lumpectomy just before my retirement, and a knee replacement, gallbladder, another rotator cuff repair, and two cataract surgeries, a retinal hemorrhage, disc, spinal stenosis operation, and a hip fracture--- all after my retirement." Dan took a deep breath before he continued. "In addition, she had COPD, sleep apnea, and sinus and migraine headaches. Later she had neck problems. Then finally she had a stroke with multiple complications. So at times I feel I am taking a time off from perpetual nursing duties."

"Wow. You were really busy nursing her. Linda needed good nurse like you all the way."

"It wasn't easy in later years, when my back pain became worse," Dan admitted. "And I had ambitious retirement plans—like doing volunteer work abroad and attending a creative writing course at the community college—but I couldn't because of the nonstop nursing chores. How about you, Lucy? You couldn't do much either. And you missed Charlie so much you cried every day, right?"

Lucy nodded. "I cried day and night until my tear glands went dry. I missed him dearly; there was this huge void around me, but I also blamed you for deserting me in the first place. And I started to wonder whatever happened to you."

"I am so sorry, Lucy. But when you were happy with Charlie, you didn't blame me for deserting you or even think about me, right?" said Dan, squeezing her hands.

Lucy didn't answer but then started to sob. "But when I visited the Choys in San Diego, I accidentally rediscovered you. Oh my God, you were still on this planet."

"Why did you use Facebook rather than calling me directly?"

"Oh, Dan. I didn't know how to approach you. I think fear of rejection was to blame. Facebook promotes friendships, so it seemed an innocuous place to start. Even then, it took me a long time and an extra courage."

After a long pause, Dan asked Lucy, "Are you okay otherwise?"

"Yes. Other than limping from chronic hip problems and occasional migraine headaches, I am okay."

"What's wrong with hip?"

"It's chronic arthritis. I'll need replacements soon."

"What about the migraines?"

"My primary thinks it's nothing but a tension headache."

"Have you had a brain MRI?"

"No, my primary doesn't think it's necessary."

"Linda had a negative MRI, but that was few years before the stroke..." Dan could not finish.

Dan changed the subject. Touching her fingers, he asked, "Why do you have so much arthritis in your fingers?"

"Occupational hazard for nurses, you know. From all the manual work."

"Like putting bedpans under seniors?"

"Of course but also IVs, CPR... and plain nursing and all the paperwork. Don't forget that I have raised four kids too."

"Four?"

"Yes, I include Charlie."

Then she said, "Let me see your hands." She quickly examined Dan's hands and said, "Wow, yours are not much different from mine. As a board-certified geriatrician, you were busy milking old flabby breasts?"

"Yes, dear. Tough job."

"Our hands are big, like farmers' hands. You had to use your hands all the time, especially checking blood pressure the old ways in rural practice, while dairy farmers were using milking machines."

She gently patted Dan's hands. "You don't wear a wedding ring."

"I had to cut it off when my arthritis got worse. How about you?"

Lucy sighed, "Same situation."

"So it's due to medical excuses and not because we are on the market again."

They had a quiet tête-à-tête on whatever topic came to mind, sometimes in half sleep, meandering through their pasts and back.

In one moment Lucy surprised Dan by asking, "What do you think about me?"

Initially Dan didn't quite understand her question. "You were happily married to my dear friend Dr. Charlie Yi. You have fabulous children and grandchildren. You excelled in your career, climbing up the proverbial ladder to break the glass ceiling, and you triumphantly returned home as a visiting professor at your alma mater, paying back all you owed them and the country. And you're healthy. What more can anyone ask?"

Lucy seemed disappointed. "That's all?"

So Dan said, "Once I saw your name on Facebook, I wanted to see you before I died, but I had this fear of rejection. But now that I am sitting next to you, I am very happy."

Lucy seemed in deep thought.

So Dan asked, "How about you?"

Now it was Lucy who seemed confused. "How about me—what?"

"Same question about me."

She sighed heavily. "When Charlie died, and I was sick and tired of being all alone, I started to wonder whatever happened to you—the guy who loved me so much and promised to marry me. Then I rediscovered you, literally out of the blue. When I realized you were a widower, I had to ask you to be a friend."

Dan felt he could hardly breathe. "A million thanks to you, Lucy... I was as surprised as you were. So we're

Facebook friends now, but anyone can be Facebook friends, right? A generic friendship, only on Facebook pages."

Lucy was quiet again, so Dan closed his eyes and tried to go to sleep.

When they were awake again, Dan said, "It's a strange fate that we didn't know we were not too far from each other. Philip and Helen came to see us in Ohio, and we went to see them in Chicago."

"As I said, you were not on my radar until after the Choys showed me your reunion pictures, but I didn't tell them we were old sweethearts."

"They live in San Diego now. Did you meet them there or in Chicago?"

"In San Diego, while visiting my middle child."

"Oh yeah? My middle guy lives in the Tahoe area and has a condo in Malibu."

After a pause, Dan said, "Looking back, I now remember meeting Charlie at least twice at medical meetings. I never knew he was married to you. Had I known about it, we could have had a huge fistfight over you. In our college alumni gatherings, families often came along, so you could have been there—and Linda too. The four of us could have met."

"It's possible, but our paths never crossed until now, not even in dreams."

"But you knew that Philip and I were classmates, and you knew we were one year behind Charlie. You could have tracked me down sooner if you wanted."

"That's true, Dan. You, too. We both were too busy

with careers, practices, and raising kids, but most of all, we were happy, living an illusion that we were living together because Charlie and Linda were our doubles. And it was only after we were widowed that we started to look beyond our fences—and here we are."

"I hope this is the beginning of something, Lucy."

On another occasion during the long flight, Lucy asked Dan, "Why are your grandkids much younger than mine?"

"It's your fault, Lucy. I had zero self-esteem for three years."

"You're the one who screwed us up, Dan. You skipped the country in haste. You abandoned me in the confusing Loop and left me all alone, devastated, and terrified."

Dan was quiet for a while. "It was for you, Lucy. They were closing in on me, so I had to hide away in hurry. I did not want to harm you and your family by simple association. As I told you then, I was against eloping because I couldn't imagine you, a delicate, naive city girl, clueless about hardship, withering in an igloo village—not just a year or two but for life. I was glad you didn't come when I saw a friend of mine going through hell."

"What happened?"

"His wife ran away after their first baby; she had postpartum depression—you know, the maternity blues… so cold, so lonesome, so far away from family, friends, and civilization."

Lucy was in deep thought. "It's no good to rehash old hurts after fourteen grandkids and eighty happy years."

"Eighty years?"

"Yes. Forty-plus years for each of us, Dr. Snail. And

no question that each of us had a good life, although not together... but almost the same as with each other."

"Why is that?"

"As we've both agreed, Charlie and Linda were our alter egos."

At another moment, Lucy asked, "How did you end up in the boondocks? In Chicago you were gung-ho about research, and you were the one who encouraged me to pursue research and teaching. I worked hard because of you. And you get the credit for any of my achievements. But you were overqualified, with four Boards, yet you ended up a country doctor."

"After three years in Canada, I went back to another fellowship when I came back to the States, but I couldn't get my research grants. I was too old, married, and a child was coming. I swore I would not starve my family, but I also wanted to go to the farthest place from the cutthroat academic competitions. So I ended up in the deepest hinterland. I guess I was burned out."

"I felt like that umpteen times. But did you like it?"

"It was one-horse town."

"What?"

"The first town had one traffic light and one cop. It also had a six-bed ICU in a small hospital that served several surrounding rural counties. I was their first-ever board-certified internist and the first ICU director with no backup, so I was very busy. But the townsfolk were wonderful. When I made occasional house calls, the patients would bring fresh eggs and freshly gutted chickens, and venison, in addition to wild ginseng roots, deer horns, and bear gallstones—all for my longevity."

"Serene too?"

"No, Professor. With twelve hundred dynamic folks, it was never serene. Rather, it was full of drama, like Peyton Place, that small town from the TV series, you know."

"Huh. What about the second town? Was it a two-horse town?"

"We had fifty thousand souls and two hospitals."

"Wow, perhaps it was ten-horse city, eh?"

"Yes, then we didn't have specialists in the ER or ICU or hospitalists, unlike nowadays, so all the practitioners had to take care of their own patients in two ERs and two ICUs, as well as inpatients at two hospitals. Although I had good cross-coverage with other solo practitioners, I was busy."

Lucy asked, "So no regrets?"

"Yes, my practice was okay, but I should have spent more time with my kids when they were young."

"What happened?"

"I was so busy I hardly saw them growing, even though we lived under one roof. Linda raised them single-handedly. In addition, I wasn't sure if our rural high school was good enough for them, so I ended up sending them to prep schools, missing them at those tender ages."

"But that was the price you had to pay for your American dream—our kids getting the best education in America, away from the war, hunger, and deprivations we had to endure."

They dozed on and off again. At times their heads

leaned sideways so their faces almost touched, and they could feel each other's breath.

At one point, Lucy held Dan's hand.

Another time, Dan found himself holding Lucy's hand—and he felt embarrassed. "Hey, Lucy. I feel guilty holding your hand."

"Why?"

"Because you're my friend's widow, and I still feel like a married man."

Lucy smiled. "You feel you're cheating?"

Dan felt as if he'd been stabbed in the heart. "Yes, Lucy... but I think you held my hand too. Did you feel ashamed?"

Blushing, she said, "Yes, initially. I thought I was with Charlie. When I realized it, I said sorry to Charlie."

"But you kept holding my hand."

"Yes, dear. Because I wanted to."

Soon they both fell asleep again, holding hands and leaning toward each other.

The flight was deep into the dark universe, and they were now more relaxed. Lucy teased, "Hey, Dan. We ended up sleeping together again, this time side by side."

Dan shot back, "Under one roof but not in the same bed."

Lucy grinned. "I'll blackmail you, saying that you slept with me. I know two things for sure about you: one is that you're grieving terribly, and the other is that you have deep pockets."

"Suit yourself. No one will believe it at our age and in our conditions."

"Our lawyers will be happy to make a few bucks, but you and I will settle it out of court with just one real kiss. I don't think you'll miss that."

"Of course not. I'd give up everything for that kiss, Professor."

On another occasion, Lucy asked, "What are you thinking, Dan?"

"Remembering."

"What about?"

"I was hoping for a colossal dowry from your blue-blood family."

"Fat chance. We were going to give you just a few skinny chickens for your farm for taking in an ugly leftover ole miss, instead of the dozen cash cows that you were hoping."

"Then those chickens laid golden eggs, you know, while cash cows spilled golden muck."

"You missed the whole shebang, Dan."

"I don't think it's too late, Lucy."

"You might get just a few dried prunes this time. How about that?"

"I'll accept anything from you. I'll use them every day."

They both dozed off again. Her head fell toward him and touched his face. He felt his pulse jumping.

"How was the sleep?" Lucy asked when Dan awoke.

"It was a million-dollar nap."

"What's that?"

"It's like baby's sleep while sucking mother's milk."

"Huh. What the heck is that?"

"All the angels sleep like that, Lucy."

"I wish I could understand what you're babbling, you codger." When Dan did not answer, Lucy said, "It looks like a very complicated sleep, with lots of brain waves crisscrossing, like a severe electrical thunderstorm."

"No, it's just a simple nice nap."

"That sounds much better, Dr. Snail. Then I'd be happy to sleep with you side by side and put you to sleep like my baby."

"That'd be great, Lucy. Hope you experience that too."

After another interval, Lucy surprised Dan by asking, "What causes aneurysms?"

Dan thought Lucy was testing him but nonetheless was concerned. "Most likely it's part of the aging process, along with high blood pressure and cholesterol buildup. The internet says it could be genetic. Twenty percent of patients do have a family history of aneurysms."

"Do you have that family history, Dan?"

"No, but back in med school, medical history textbooks said syphilis was a leading cause of aneurysm in younger groups, but that was way before the penicillin era."

Lucy feigned surprise. "Syphilis?"

"Yes, we don't see it too often nowadays."

Lucy snickered. "Maybe you were a playboy when you were young."

"Oh yes, Don Juan was my best childhood chum."

The long flight was still chugging along. The navigation screen showed they were now just over the point of no return. Dan saw Lucy was awake but in deep thought. Soon he whispered, "I'm glad that so far our reunion has been good."

"Not so traumatic?"

"The other way around, Lucy. I had this incredible fear of rejection before sending you my first email."

"Nervous, like when you asked me for our first date?"

"Yes. But thanks to your magnanimity, I feel so good so far."

"But I don't," Lucy snapped, pouting.

"Why? So I've failed you after all. I'm very sorry. I'll jump up to the business class. I know they still have several seats available." Dan tried to unbuckle his seatbelt.

Holding his hand, Lucy said, "Oh no, Dan. It's not rejection." After a long pause, she said, "It's déjà vu. Just like the first time, I know I am falling. I had to take you on this journey. God told me to do so. This is fate. But now I'm going to lose you the second time around." Lucy now was sobbing.

Dan realized that Lucy now understood how bad his prognosis was, unlike at the San Francisco airport, when she tried to sound upbeat. "Oh Lucy, I'm so sorry. If you don't feel comfortable with me one way or another, you just tell me to back off. I'll be okay, as long as we keep our Facebook friendship."

Still holding Dan's hand, she said, "As I've said ad nauseam, it's not rejection, you moron."

"I am not asking you for anything but friendship... no strings attached."

"Friendship between us is not that simple, Dr. Snail."

"You're saying that falling in a friendship is as scary

as falling in love? Then let's do that thing—carpe diem—avoiding all the storms, perfect or semi-perfect."

Still sobbing, Lucy said, "I just don't know how this journey will end, let alone how soon."

"Yogi Berra also said the future is hard to predict." Dan hoped to cheer her up but getting no response, he said, "Oh, my sweetheart, everything is in God's hands. Relax. Let's just stay as Facebook friends, okay?"

"You just don't understand, Dr. Snail."

"You can give me a six-month extension on Facebook friendship, just like my doctors are doing."

"It might make things worse. Regardless, this will break my heart for the third time."

"How?"

"I lost you before, then Charlie, and now I'll lose you again. I don't think I can handle another loss."

They clasped their hands tightly, leaning their heads closer together, and soon drifted off to sleep.

An hour later, Lucy said, "I slept well, just like baby. It was your million-dollar nap."

"Wow. It sounds like enlightenment."

"Yes, Dan."

"Ecstasy?"

"No, but I was euphoric, as if we were in nirvana. Holding your hand brought our ruby romance back."

"Ruby romance?"

"Yes, forty-some-year-old love."

"We were platonic," said Dan.

"That's why it has survived all these years and resurrected."

Now the flight was approaching Japan. Dan went to the restroom to brush his teeth and shave. Lucy also went to restroom and came out with fresh makeup on. When she settled back into her seat, Dan grabbed her hand and said, "You are a confirmed Christian, while I'm only a semi, so I'd like to ask you to hold an official prayer session."

"For what, Dan?"

"To say sorry to Linda and Charlie."

"Yes, I've done it already, but let's do it together."

They prayed together, holding hands.

As the plane approached Seoul, Dan wrote his local phone number and address on a piece of paper. "Lucy, it's been very nice of you to let me tag along on this journey. I wished this journey would never end. We need another one or two to catch up on each other."

Lucy was impassive.

Dan continued. "I know you're busy, but I wish we could have a brief rendezvous in Seoul, if possible."

She nodded, surprising Dan. Putting the paper into her purse, Lucy smiled. "Dan, you're as nervous as when you were asking me for our second date."

Once at the airport, they walked together through customs and immigration. Dan noticed she was traveling light, just like he was, and did not need his help. Before going out into the waiting area, Lucy gave him a peck on the cheek.

CHAPTER 4
Seoul Grand Hyatt

IN SEOUL, DAN STAYED WITH his youngest sister. He was anxious to hear from Lucy, but she didn't call him for one full week. He couldn't call her because he didn't have her phone number, but Dan was confident Lucy would call him. Finally, just two days before coming home, Lucy called. His sister answered and handed the phone to him.

"It's for you, big brother. This lady says she's your old friend. I didn't know you had a girlfriend in Seoul. She sounds pleasant and cheerful."

Obviously, her Seoul dialect was flawless, with no trace of an American accent. Lucy said she had a couple of hours free the next morning and wondered if Dan could come out for brunch. Dan was elated.

The Seoul Grand Hyatt was a nice place on the side of Namsan Hill. Lucy was waiting for him in the lobby, wearing her red scarf and red cap again. Dan was wearing his red baseball cap. They hugged.

At the restaurant, Lucy said, "I haven't seen so many Koreans in one place in a long time."

"Did you visit your alma mater, Lucy?"

"Yes. They asked me to lecture. So I spoke to the whole junior and senior classes."

"Very proud of you for doing that. I'm sure they were proud of you too."

"Have you done any sightseeing?" Dan asked.

"I'm not interested in sightseeing," Lucy said stiffly.

"Not me either, but last year I stayed one night at the President Hotel for our reunion dinner."

"In City Square?" Lucy asked.

"Yes. The City Square looked so small compared to when we rioted there in 4/19." He was referring to the Student Revolution of April 19, 1960, that toppled Dr. Syngman Rhee's thirteen- year authoritarian rules.

"Yes, then we had to rise up for our nascent democracy, demanding a new election," said Lucy. "But soon we all became helpless victims of its powerful aftershocks. You told me that after the revolution, the new government jailed your dad, and you guys had a really hard time, and they were after you ever since."

"Yes, but that's history now, including the tear gas. We used to cry even when we were in a tea house; remember that?"

They were reminiscing about the chaotic postriot period, when Korea was a nation of tears from the indiscriminate use of tear gas on the incessant street demonstrations. Gut-wrenching anarchy eventually led to the coup d'état on May 16, 1961.

Lucy asked, "How was the wedding?"

Dan said, "The present-day Korean wedding was more American, with only a few Korean features, and the urban wedding was very efficient, like an assembly line, with five weddings going on smoothly at the same time. The dining hall was huge, with large flat-screen TVs around the walls, showing all five weddings at the same time so that we could watch them while eating. As soon as we finished eating, we were rushed out, and the next group was herded in. I missed the traditional village wedding."

"How was the food?" Lucy asked.

"Excellent! One of the best Korean buffets I have ever eaten."

"That's a sign of progress."

"Korea is much richer. People are healthier and taller by one head than when we were here," Dan agreed.

"Have you seen everyone in your family?" Lucy asked.

"Yes. Now I have only three sisters. How about you, Lucy?"

"I have two brothers and one sister here. Their children are old now. Their grandkids are all complete strangers to me," Lucy said, disgusted.

"No one has died?" Dan was inquisitive.

"Luckily, no one yet."

"My brother died a long time ago from chronic hepatitis, but the others are healthy. My brother's family is doing well. Kids are successful."

Dan asked Lucy, "You have visited your parents' tombs, right?"

"Of course. It was the first thing I did. I said goodbye to them. How about you, Dan?"

"Same... in the village. So now you have closed some nostalgic chapters in Korea."

"Yes, but how did you know I came for that?"

"Lucy. It was written all over your face in the San Francisco airport."

Lucy was moved, "You too, Dan."

"Yes, I came here last year, and I came back again this year. I think this trip could be my last."

Lucy asked, "Your aneurysm prompted this trip."

Dan was surprised, "Yes, and the wedding was an excuse. It's my last wedding to attend in Korea, and funerals will start soon, but I don't know if I can... I mean physically. I don't think my siblings could attend my funeral either."

"Too sad, Dan."

"I have a personal question. You'll be buried next to Charlie in the States, right?"

"Absolutely. My kids and grandkids are all in the States. How about you?"

"Same. We don't belong to our old country anymore."

Lucy nodded in agreement. "Dan, we are closing a big chapter."

While drinking tea after the brunch, Lucy said, "I wish I could go home with you."

Dan was surprised. "You're homesick already?"

"Yes, but also I want to fly back sitting next to you."

"Aha. You miss that million-dollar nap?"

"Yes, it was romantic."

"You mean two confused seniors holding hands, drooling, dozing on and off?" They both laughed at that. "That's a special privilege of flying economy class," Dan told her.

Lucy nodded but quickly added, "You should fly first class on the way home."

Dan was surprised. "Why? Are you rejecting me now?"

Making a face, Lucy said, "I don't want you to get confused and hold the next person's hand." Dan seemed perplexed, so Lucy declared, "Besides, you deserve better treatment for yourself after working so hard for your kids and the IRS for fifty years."

"Okay, boss. I'll be careful, but only if I have passed your initial evaluation and only if you give me a six-month extension on our Facebook friendship."

"Yes, Dan."

"You mean I get to see you again soon?" Dan said, eagerly anticipating. When he saw her nodding, he thought this was too good to be true. "I'm honored. It changes my whole perspective. I wouldn't mind going home all the way while handcuffed," said Dan, holding Lucy's hands.

As they were winding down their rendezvous, Dan gave Lucy one each of his two books. "These are souvenirs. I don't expect you to read them."

"Oh, thank you, Dan. I'll keep them as my treasures and try to read."

At the lobby, they took a couple of selfies with their red hats on and hugged for a long time. Lucy pecked Dan on the cheek before parting.

Chapter 5
After Seoul

O NE WEEK AFTER LUCY RETURNED home, Dan sent her their selfie pictures of them wearing their red hats in front of the Seoul Grand Hyatt. He captioned them "Red-Capped Facebook Comrades" and wrote, "Hope you had a very happy reunion with your grandkids." Lucy called Dan soon after that, saying everything went well.

In spite of his initial overwhelming fear of rejection, he was glad that their reconnection went well, and he hoped to see Lucy soon again. Dan was glad that he had not concealed his health problems. Rather, he knew it was his duty to inform Lucy before starting a relationship with her, even their *harmless* Facebook friendship. He would not have blamed Lucy if she decided to shy away.

One day on his way home from a weekend stay in Aspen, Colorado, Dan turned on his car radio but heard only static, as he was driving through the Rocky Mountains, where the radio reception was very poor. As he continued to scan the radio waves, he soon found a steady FM station. Listening to it carefully, he was surprised it was airing a medical melodrama, and he was more surprised when he learned their patient had exactly the same conditions as his—aortic stenosis and ascending aortic aneurysm. He stopped his car on shoulder of the road so he wouldn't lose the radio signal and listened intently to the entire story.

The patient was a sixty-year-old woman who suffered from fainting spells and chest pain, all from severe aortic stenosis, but her big aneurysm was quiescent. After an eight-hour surgery, she awoke in the intensive care unit, listening to metallic heart sounds from her new heart valve. It was so loud anyone could hear it, even without a stethoscope. Being a radio show, they amplified her heart sound to the maximum for one full minute before fading it out. The announcer then said that the heart noise eventually subsided about in a year, and everything else went well.

Dan's immediate reaction was déjà vu of his earlier med student days, when he was learning heart sounds. It also told him how precarious his health was. He was glad that someone with the same conditions as his survived a lengthy heart operation, although this patient was much younger.

It was an astonishing experience. He learned about his own medical problems from a totally unexpected source, and location—a radio medical melodrama on the high Continental Divide atop the Rocky Mountains.

Naturally, Dan was more concerned about his follow-up tests. The first was an echocardiogram. The aneurysm, the silent killer, was bigger, but the aortic valve was about the same. Later, Dan's surgeon ordered a CT scan to get a more accurate measurement of the aneurysm.

Two weeks later, Dan called Lucy. "I saw my heart surgeon yesterday," he said. "Basically it's good news. He said my aneurysm was only slightly larger than two years ago, at 4.8 centimeters. It didn't grow faster. He said the critical size for preemptive surgery is now 5.5 centimeters, not 5 centimeters."

Lucy had a hard time taking in this information. "Could you speak slowly to a grandma?"

"Sorry. As of now, I have seven years to the surgery."

Lucy sighed with relief. "That's really wonderful news, Dan. Each extra year at our age is like ten extra years when young. So the only thing you have to do is carpe diem, eh?"

"Yes, dear. I think I'll go to church again."

"For what? You said you started going last year."

"Yes, I did for a while but then stopped."

"Oh my. Still, the Christian burial is what you want, right?"

"Oh no, Lucy. This time I want to thank God for giving me some extra time to enjoy our Facebook friendship."

"Oh. You're so sweet. God bless you, Dan."

The following week Dan called Lucy again. "Hey, would you be interested in going on a cruise with me?"

Lucy was so surprised she could not answer him right away.

"I wanted to go on a cruise for a long time and have saved money," Dan explained, "but I hated to go alone. But after the Seoul trip, it occurred to me that we both could use a cruise, and I've wanted to ask you for some time, but I again was scared of rejection."

"Oh no. I'd be happy to go on a cruise with you, Dan," Lucy responded without any hesitation. "In fact, I was thinking of inviting you for a long weekend trip. We have so many stories to catch up, but you're as nervous as when you asked me for our third date."

Dan did not know if he should cry or laugh.

Lucy was quick to ask, "When and where would we go? I'm scared of hurricanes."

"The one I have in mind is in early April to the western Caribbean, from Galveston, Texas. It's not in hurricane season. It's also right after spring break for most schools— college kids are more dangerous than hurricane or sharks."

"Okay. It sounds great, but let me talk to my kids."

One week later, when Lucy said yes, Dan asked, "What did your kids say about you going on a cruise with me? Were they upset?"

"No, everyone said to go ahead. They said it would be great for my brain."

"They just wanted to get rid of you for a week for their own peace, but what do they think is wrong with your brain?"

"They think I've gone irreversibly cuckoo since Charlie's funeral."

"All right, then. You could come to Denver first, or I could go to Chicago."

"Either way is okay, but what about the cabin?" Lucy was one step ahead of Dan.

"It's usually one stateroom with double occupancy, as you know, but we could get two."

"I don't think it's necessary, Dan. We can share a room. It's more convenient for two limping seniors, helping each other."

That surprised Dan. "You're no longer a shy Korean girl anymore."

"Oh, heaven's sake. I'm now a practical American grandma—in love."

That shocked Dan. "Are we in love? You didn't tell me that. Are you sure?"

"Positive. You're so dense that you didn't catch it, or maybe you've forgotten it already. You need hearing aids, or a brain transplant, or both—as soon as possible."

"People will think that we're a married couple anyway," said Dan sheepishly.

"Don't be so shy, Dan. Tell the truth—that we're seniors in love. Having two rooms between two old sweethearts is totally absurd. Who are we kidding but ourselves?"

"Okay, Lucy. You also want a million-dollar nap, holding hands together?"

"Of course. We'll have just one room for now, Dan." Lucy was eager to end the discussion on room issues.

"All right, Professor. We can change that at any time."

After confirming the cruise, it occurred to Dan that he should visit Lucy so he could meet her kids and grandkids before the cruise.

When he asked her, she said, "You sound like a young boy eager to meet your girlfriend's parents. My kids will wonder what kind of guy their mother is hanging around, right? But I don't need their permission. On the other hand, seeing their mom dating someone too soon after their dad's death might hurt their feelings. Let me think about it, Dan."

A week later, she called. "Hey, Dan. I think it's too early."

CHAPTER 6
Denver

L UCY FLEW TO DENVER TWO days before the cruise. After coming home from the airport, Dan took her to the master bedroom.

Lucy looked at him with surprise. "This was obviously Linda's bedroom. How can I sleep here?"

"No problem, Lucy. It's our guest room now."

"Guest room?"

"Yes, after retiring to Denver, we didn't have another room large enough with a bath so we'd been using this as our guest room. So this is your room for now, as my guest."

"Where will you sleep?"

"Oh, I have my own room. It's my study, but we used to call it *on-call* room. It's at the end of the hallway, but it's so messy I can't show it to you."

"On-call room?" Lucy asked.

"Yes, during my solo practice days, my phones and beeper rang continuously, twenty-four/seven, for forty years, causing me to jump up on each ring and beep. Linda couldn't stand it, so we eventually had to sleep far apart."

"I understand," Lucy sympathized. "Charlie's life was not much different, but he had good coverage."

"I don't have a beeper now," Dan said, "and my phone calls are mostly from family, although I still get enough robocalls."

Lucy insisted on seeing his room, so he had no choice. After looking around for a few moments, she said, "Wow! It's a nice, cozy cubbyhole but lots of wires and cables, like spider webs. You have an oversized cluttered desk, a tiny filing cabinet, and a mini-bookcase, but it's bare—no books, certificates, pictures, or memorabilia. How come?"

"After my near-fatal heart attack, I was convinced I was going to die within a year," Dan explained, "so I began to clean up. My children didn't want any of my stuff, so I trashed everything—pictures, color slides, diplomas, specialty certificates, books, medical magazines, and gizmos, as well as my electronic files, including daily journals, essays, and others."

"Oh no!" Lucy was horrified.

"The most difficult thing was giving away my core mementos—my tattered black bag with my old tools of the trade, my cello, and an ancient microscope. I was happy when my daughter took those pieces." He smiled at Lucy: "I guess you still have all your books and memorabilia." She nodded. "Still, I became complacent soon after my last CT scan. It occurred to me that I might linger for a few more years, so I started to digitize some of the remaining pictures and unfinished manuscripts on USB flash drives."

"Why?" Lucy asked.

"It's a kind of a time capsule. Rather than trashing

everything in a landfill, I wanted a couple of flash drives to put into my urn and take them on my journey."

"Oh, it's a great idea," Lucy agreed, "but only if it works."

"I could use pyramid, considering the amount of treasures I've piled up."

"But the Bible says ashes to ashes," Lucy reminded him.

Dan feigned surprise. "I was born bare-handed, but you were born with a silver spoon in your mouth."

"Huh, I forgot about it. I'll sneak one into my urn and hope I'm born with it again in the next world."

Lucy soon changed the subject. "Can I sleep here tonight? I may not feel so guilty."

"You're more than welcome, but do you want to sleep alone or with me?" Dan asked with a crooked smile.

"I meant switching rooms, but either way. In case you've forgotten, we almost got married, and we did sleep together several times without any incident. You're a harmless guy to sleep with."

"Harmless? Like a eunuch? Neutered?"

"No, totally inhibited, even without castration." That brought healthy laughter from both of them. Lucy continued. "We slept side by side on the plane and few times totally naked in our halcyon days."

"Halcyon days?"

"Yes, those simple, untroubled days when we didn't have to spill our tears."

"Then I'll have to change the linens and bed cover."

"Oh no. Don't bother. I also want to get reacquainted with your scents."

"Although it looks small, this bed was good for two."

"For you and Linda?"

"Yes. Linda used to sneak in."

"I might do that tonight."

"You're scaring me, Lucy. As an old man living alone, I'm used to sleeping all alone, and it would be tough to sleep with someone, especially such a beautiful lady like you." Lucy just blushed. "Also, I snore terribly."

"Ha! Don't try to scare me off. I snore too, and half of US seniors have sleep apnea, they say."

Soon Dan gave Lucy a tour of the house. "It's a small house, but it's too much for me. I was going to get a studio apartment."

"Our home is way too big also."

"It will be painful to sell and move out, Lucy."

He then showed her the hot tub on his deck.

"Can I use it tonight?" Lucy asked.

Dan nodded. "Absolutely. It will be good for your tired muscles after a long flight."

They went to an Italian restaurant for supper. On the way home, they stopped by a supermarket to pick up groceries, because Dan had nothing but canned foods and instant noodles. It was dark already.

"It might be a good time for you to use the hot tub before you get too tired," Dan suggested, and Lucy agreed.

When they were in the hot tub, their toes touched from time to time, making Dan's heartbeat jump. It was a very nice feeling to be with Lucy, but Dan felt as if his wife, Linda, was with him, and he had a hard time refraining from kissing her.

After a shower, they sat on the sofa and had wine. Soon Lucy said, "I think that wine is making me dopey."

Dan took her to the bedroom. After kissing her on cheek, he went downstairs to watch the news, but soon he fell asleep while sitting on the sofa. He woke up in the middle of night and went to his own bed.

Dan was in the living room the next morning when Lucy came downstairs. She cooked eggs and bacon, and Dan prepared coffee.

"It's nice to have you around, Lucy. I feel I'm back at your apartment in Chicago for a Sunday power brunch."

"You miss the slight female touch, eh?"

"Of course. This is my first real breakfast in many years. Living alone in old age sucks."

"I feel your pain, Dan. Why do we have to get old and lose our mates? Aging sucks. This is not our golden age but a hell."

"So our golden age is gone, or did it bypass us?" asked Dan.

"Our golden age was when our kids were small. That was when we enjoyed every day of life, watching them growing up... These are our twilight years—full of despair, everything falling apart."

They spent morning not doing much. In midafternoon they went to town to a gym center and exercised together.

In the evening, they went to Dan's younger son Jim's for dinner. Dan's daughter, Anna, came with her family, and all five grandchildren were there. Another son was in

California. Dan told Lucy that Jim was a vice president at a bank, and Anna was with a brokerage firm.

Dan had told Jim about Lucy few weeks earlier, saying that Lucy was an old friend in his training days and now a college friend's widow.

"Be careful, Dad. Companionship is okay, but otherwise, things could get complicated."

"We're just friends," Dan assured him.

Dan's children were shocked and worried about their dad dating, perhaps far more than they worried about their own children dating. His kids might have gone ballistic had he brought a young chick, but perhaps an older date was more tolerable to the family—although they preferred that he not date at all. He was definitely a huge liability to the family.

Lucy had a good time. Kids and grandkids were polite and didn't say much, but Dan knew that they were watching them closely.

Once they were back at Dan's, Lucy said, "I liked your grandkids."

"They will think about Linda whenever they see you, just like I do."

"What do you mean?"

"I think of Linda whenever I see you or hear your voice."

"It's the same for me with Charlie and you," Lucy said with a sigh.

"Did your kids complain about your going on a cruise with a girlfriend?" Lucy poked a fun at Dan.

"Oh yes. Wasting my estate money, et cetera, but now they all know I have saved money from my allowances.

That night Lucy told Dan to pack all his medications for the cruise.

"Yes, boss. I am all set. You too?"

She nodded. "Yes, I have common medications that seniors take—for cholesterol, high blood pressure, depression, and to help me sleep.

"Sorry that you have to take medication for depression. I hope that soon you won't need it. Depression is more common in single seniors than people realize." When Lucy asked about his medications, Dan said, "They're similar to yours, but I take a few more that massive heart attack survivors take, like a blood thinner, but I don't take anything for depression or sleeping."

"Do you take nitrates?" Lucy asked. Nitrates were commonly used heart medications.

Dan promptly answered, "No, but I carry a small bottle all the times. Why do you ask?"

"As your traveling nurse companion, I should know everything, just in case." She gave him a lopsided smile: "You know, if you take long-acting nitrates, you cannot take blue pills."

"Blue pills? I don't need it."

"Because you're still naturally strong?" Lucy asked right back.

"No, Professor. I don't have any use of it."

They both laughed and went back to other medication issues.

"Are you tolerating medications okay, Dan?"

"Yes, so far so good. You also want to know about coffee, right? I used to drink two to three pots a day in my heydays, but now I am allowed only two cups of decaf. The best news is that I can drink a bottle of red wine a day."

"Oh no. Your cardiologist probably said it's okay to drink it once in a while, not a whole bottle every day."

Then Lucy asked, "Are you taking your cane with you?"

"I use retractable walking sticks when I travel by air because they fit into my carry-on bag. How about you? Did you bring yours?"

"Yes, a stick. We'll need them on shore as well as on the ship."

After a while, Dan asked, "All done checking me into your world? You're very thorough. I'd like to say one word, off the record, with your permission." When Lucy nodded, he said, "You're good-looking."

"Oh, stop it, you dirty old man."

The evening air was cool, but they decided to use the hot tub. After showering, they sat in living room, sipping red wine. Soon Dan pulled Lucy to him and kissed her hard. She responded, and they stayed that way for a long time. That was their first kiss in forty-five years.

Dan said meekly, "I'm very sorry, Lucy. I'm a confused dirty old man."

"Aha. You thought you were kissing Linda while stealing kisses from me, you old bastard." She pretended to slap his face.

With his head down, Dan said, "Sorry. I got mixed up."

Before Dan finished, Lucy grabbed him by neck and kissed him hard. "Don't be so sorry, Dan, you idiot. I thought I was kissing Charlie too."

"Ah, are we both barking up the wrong trees?" Dan asked.

"Not really. We're just confused, temporarily." Lucy smiled.

"But we prayed to God, Charlie, and Linda to forgive us for cheating on our spouses."

"No, Dan, our late spouses—they're now deceased," Lucy corrected him calmly.

They woke up early for their 8:00 a.m. flight and stopped at McDonald's on the way to the airport. At security, Dan was searched all over. While tying up his shoelaces at a bench where Lucy was waiting, Dan said, "Sorry. I was clumsy. I had my nitro bottle in my passport pouch around my neck and the x-ray machine caught it."

"You are doing just fine," Lucy said.

"I definitely am getting more forgetful. Things like this are getting on my nerves."

"Don't worry, Dan. All the seniors get frustrated at the security. I had some issues too."

Dan's eyebrows shot up in surprise. "What issues?"

Lucy shook her head, reluctant to reveal it now. "I'll tell you later."

The flight to Houston was short. Lucy held Dan's hand, and he noted that her hand was warm. The bus ride to Galveston took two hours because of the heavy weekend traffic.

CHAPTER 7
Cruise

WHILE BOARDING, LUCY SAID, "THIS is my fourth cruise."

"This is my third and could be my last," said Dan.

They went to their stateroom first. It was on the ship's bow and starboard side and had a balcony. It was spacious, with a double bed, a sofa, and a desk. Lucy took the ocean side of the bed.

"This side is closer to the bathroom—good for an old man," said Dan, not realizing they'd soon squabble over their sleeping arrangement. They both sent texts home: "On board. No internet or phone services. No news is good news."

They were hungry so they decided to go to the buffet restaurant on the top deck. Realizing that their room was some distance away from the elevators, they decided to use walking sticks whenever they went out. They ate sandwiches while watching the harbor through the window.

After the mandatory evacuation drill, they explored the ship. On deck five, they saw many shops and bars. It was obviously the "downtown" of this floating city. Then they checked the gym areas before going to the open upper deck, where they watched the ship leave the harbor.

That evening, they decided to retire early after a long day. Lucy took a shower first. When Dan sauntered into the room after a leisurely shower, he was shocked to see Lucy wearing nothing but her underwear and bra, resting on the bed, facing the ocean side. Clearly, she was relaxed and unfazed by naked Dan, who scurried around, trying to dress in a hurry.

After grabbing his clothes, Dan rushed back to the bathroom. When he came back to the room, Lucy now was watching TV, still on her minimal clothing. Dan sat down on the sofa and watched the TV too, but he couldn't help but glance at Lucy, half-naked, just a few feet away.

She was beautiful, but she was so calm and acting so natural, only then did it dawn on him that Lucy had to be in a trance. It was surreal, but he decided not to wake her up and instead enjoyed ogling her.

Sometime later, Dan broke the silence, "CNN is the only news channel, Professor."

"That's fine with me," said Lucy. Dan still didn't know if she was in a trance. He felt sorry for Lucy if she was out of her mind after suffering so much grief, but she was obviously unalarmed and felt safe with him. Dan smirked, remembering Lucy's saying that he was a safe guy to sleep with... like one who was neutered.

Dan soon heard Lucy snoring. He put the bedcover on her because the room was rather cool with the air conditioning. Later, he put a cushion behind his back and fell asleep sitting on the sofa.

When he awoke few hours later, Lucy was sitting next to him, holding his hand. She was still wearing minimal clothing, making his heart skip a few beats. He thought Lucy had arrived next to him while sleepwalking.

"You slept on while sitting on the sofa?" she said. "Must have been uncomfortable." It was now clear that Lucy was not in a trance.

"No, Lucy, it was good. I'm used to sleeping like this. It's my *on-call* mode."

"You should sleep in the bed. Our bed is big enough for two."

"I'll sleep here tonight, Lucy. You are my honorary sister," said Dan, smiling.

"Sister? We're sweethearts..." Lucy murmured, but at that moment she caught Dan ogling her and barked, "Why are you looking at me like a wolf?"

"Oh, um." Caught off guard, Dan just blushed.

"We've seen each other naked and even slept together naked a few times," she reminded him.

Red-faced, Dan mumbled, "Sorry. I couldn't help myself. You're so sexy."

"Oh, shut up, you dirty old man. We can sleep together, cuddling like puppies."

"On top of one another, like when we were young?"

"Side by side, like in the airplane to Seoul."

"You're too dangerous to sleep with, Lucy."

"I won't bite you. You and I know our cuddling is way overdue. Forty-five years to be exact. I want to sleep holding you tight, day and night. I came here for that. You did too, Dan. Be honest."

That shocked Dan. He lifted her onto his lap. After

kissing her for a long time, he said, "Nice holding you like this, Lucy. Two of us cuddling in a secret tryst on a cruise ship, far away from all the grieving. My dream has come true, finally, but I just don't know how to handle this."

Ignoring him, Lucy whispered into Dan's ear, "We had a long day. I'm aching all over. Let's move to the bed and get ourselves comfortable."

"Lucy, darling, as much as I want it, and even after a forty-five-year wait, sleeping together tonight seems a tad too early." When Lucy pouted, Dan said, "I have a great idea." When Lucy looked up at him, Dan said, "For tonight, let's sleep my way, on the sofa, just as we are now. It's to warm up ourselves, but tomorrow we will sleep in bed, your way."

"No way, Jose. It's ridiculous to sleep here with a nice empty bed just few feet away. There isn't one iota of difference between this and cuddling in bed. Also, I can't stay this way because of my hips. Let's go to bed now."

They argued, and it went on and on, with neither one yielding. Finally, Lucy proposed to settle the dispute by thumb-wrestling, as they used to do when they were young. Lucy tried hard, but after losing three to two, she conceded defeat—but she refused to sleep on his lap or on the sofa.

Lucy frowned. "Perhaps you misunderstand my intentions. You're still too shy; a worrywart, a born loser."

"Story of my life."

Lucy kissed him on his cheek and gave him a pillow and blanket so that Dan could sleep on the sofa.

Early in the morning, when Lucy saw Dan waking up, she came over and sat at the edge of the sofa. "How did you sleep?" she asked him.

"Okay. How about you?"

"Not too bad, but I missed you. We slept in the same room but far apart. It wasn't fair."

"Aha. Because you missed that million-dollar nap?"

"Yes. That was the best sleep I've ever had." Looking straight in Dan's eyes, Lucy proclaimed, "This cruise is our quasi honeymoon. So we have to sleep together. And sleeping together doesn't mean that we have to make love. No sex—I promise—so no guilt trip for you. Also, I want pillow talk."

"What about?"

"Everything, including geishas."

"Geishas?"

"Yes, I want to know how you two idiots lost your virginity."

"Oh my. We just drank and passed out as always, nothing else."

"On a geisha's bosom, right? Can we talk about it now, please? Pillow talk while caressing is the best part of intimacy. I'm still sleepy. Let's go sleep, Dan. It's my turn, so we have to go to bed now."

"You got permission?"

"What the hell are you talking about, Dr. Snail?"

"Charlie's permission to cuddle."

"Yes, don't you remember? We both prayed together to God, Charlie, and Linda. They all said whatever we did was up to us, saying that they were the ones who put us together so we could enjoy companionship until we meet them again."

"Oh my. I didn't know that's how we got together. I

thought we were asking them to forgive us for holding hands."

"You're forgetful. Senile already."

Dan was in a deep thought before he said, "Okay. Then this will be our first time to sleep with someone other than the ones we are married to."

That infuriated Lucy. She grabbed Dan's neck and shouted at him. "Wake up, Dan. There is no scandal here, you dope. We were married, but we both were widowed. Even that was three years ago. We do have death certificates to prove it, you idiot. Besides, you and I were old sweethearts, and we are here to renew it, Dr. Snail."

"So we're a card-carrying widow or widower, eh?" Dan chuckled, but Lucy ignored him.

"I'm tired of all the hogwash. It's pitiful... Can I kiss you now?"

That was when Dan grabbed her, and after a long, lingering kiss, he whispered, "You win, Lucy. Your charm is enough to make a blind old monk go crazy, you Lorelei. I'll surrender but with one condition."

"What is it, you old monk?" She was now smiling, with both arms around his neck.

"I'll take all the blame if anything goes wrong, but I don't want to lose our Facebook friendship."

"I solemnly swear to God. I grant you our Facebook friendship for another six months, no matter what happens to us in the next hour."

While walking to the bed, Dan murmured, "We're starting it pretty early in day."

"Babies are conceived every minute on the Love Boat,

Dr. Snail. With a full moon still shining and also with high tide, babies conceived in this hour should be the best."

Soon Lucy started to kiss him all over. She was now red-hot, with all cylinders in every cell cranking. "Oh my. I've missed this all these years. This is where we were in Chicago, and this is where we're restarting," she declared. "I can tell that you like this as much as I do."

Soon they tickled, giggled, and laughed, just like when they were young. Dan said, "Your bedside manner hasn't changed, Professor."

"Yours either, Dr. Snail."

Then they were silent for a long time as they locked their lips, exploring each other's heart and soul.

Sometime later, Dan lamented, "Definitely senior love, especially between a grandma and a grandpa, should go in gentle, slow motion."

Lucy snapped right back, "If we go any slower than now, we both will fall asleep in a minute." When Dan seemed to be million miles away for a second, Lucy grinned. "Aha. You're back to your born-loser mentality again, refusing to seduce me."

"Huh. We had mutual nonaggression treaty, Lucy."

"What the heck are you talking about?"

"We promised not to cross the bridge of no return until our official honeymoon."

"I wasn't fond of that treaty."

"But it was your smart creation, the original ground rules for our puppy love."

Soon Lucy was aggressive again. "Now that I've caught you after your forty-five-year AWOL, I'm going to punish you to the maximum by kissing you as much as possible before you ever desert me again."

"Oh my. You're taking no prisoners."

Sometime later, Lucy spoke in a conspirator's whisper: "I have special gift for you, Dan." When his eyes widened, Lucy said with a mischievous smile, "I have some blue and pink pills, just in case."

Stunned, Dan asked, "What? How did you get them? From a Canadian mail order?"

"I borrowed one bottle each from my son's sample room," Lucy said sheepishly.

"Oh my. After all, you are well prepared for our honeymoon."

"Yes. They are just in case we both develop a dying wish."

"I'm already dying for that."

"But it has to be consensual. And that means I decide when to use them. And it also means you have to be extra nice to me."

Then Lucy kissed him all over again. She still was red-hot, but soon she moaned, "Oh, Dan. I hate to do this, but we have to cool down now. Otherwise, we'll cross the *bridge*."

"Don't go any further than your comfort zone, Lucy. We'll cross the bridge later, sometime soon, holding hands."

"Oh, Dan, thank you."

"Even in my foggy mind, I know that friendship and companionship are far more important than sex at our age. Platonic love could be ideal."

"Not really, Dan. Platonic love is not enough for semi-legit partners like us."

"Semi-legit?"

"Yes, we're long-lost sweethearts. Now that we both are widowed, I've reclaimed you back as mine. But you're still grieving terribly and very remorseful at having brought an aging old flame on this cruise."

That stunned Dan. He whispered, "Not true. But how about you, my sweet Swiss Cheese? You're still sticking to Ten Regrets and Ten Commandments at the same time, and you're afraid of crossing the bridge, the same as when you were single."

In Dan's opinion, the Confucian Ten Regrets in East were like what the Ten Commandments were in West.

When Lucy pouted without answering, Dan said, "It's more than the grieving. I feel it's like *incest*."

"What? Incest?"

"Yes, Lucy, because I feel you're my long-lost dear twin sister, rather than a long-lost girlfriend. In addition, you're my dear friend's widow. I can share your soul with Charlie but not your body."

"Not true, Dan. I make my own decisions, now that Charlie is gone. You were my first love. I had a crush on you then, as now. No rush, but our time is coming up... very soon. To be truthful, we both want it, and I'm almost ready, and you're only one step behind me."

Lucy was quiet for a while but soon started to hyperventilate and shouted. "You're a pathetic, perpetually grieving widower! You cannot dwell on it forever. Get a grip, Dan! Rewind the clock back to our halcyon days. Delete the forty-five-year hiatus." After taking a deep breath, Lucy continued. "Here we're nothing but long-lost sweethearts, reigniting our puppy love on the Love Boat. Don't ruin our honeymoon. So forget the notion of incest." She was fuming and out of breath when she finished her tirade.

"Delete it?"

"Yes, completely."

"How can we delete our children, grandchildren, or even our deceased mates?"

"Oh shoot. Not them. Just rewind around them." When Dan did not grasp her idea, Lucy lectured him again: "We'd been bosom buddies and then soul mates for a long time. We'll soon be part-time lovers, but even with the best of intentions, we won't be there soon enough. So to be pragmatic, we should call ourselves *semi-lovers* for now and enjoy it."

"Semi-lovers? Sounds like semi-pregnant. Doesn't it have to be all or none?"

"Relax, Dan. It's just an intimate companionship."

Dan was now completely confused but also fascinated with all the new *semi* things. So Dan said, "Please educate me regarding what this semi-lover thing is all about, Professor."

"It's about love, not sex. It's simple old fashioned puppy love. Semi-lovers can kiss and cuddle naked but no sex."

"Not a complete package?" Dan was confused but soon said, "I'm now getting some idea, Professor. We are *live* teddy bears."

"You're a smart boy. Very close, Dan."

"Also, we could call ourselves senior puppy-lovers but also quasi lovers, cuddlers, snugglers, or even shy strange-bedfellows."

"Don't make things complicated, Dan. I prefer

semi-lovers, although it's not perfect. We can physically enjoy each other as much, even without sex, so we'll hold it off for now, until we both are ready, my sweetheart. We'll take a cold shower *before* jumping into bed naked." Lucy erupted into jolting laughter of self-delight.

"A cold shower seems a fair trade, but why *before*?"

"Oh, Dan. It's to cleanse us of our guilt complexes." Lucy paused. "I think that's how much we can do for now. To be honest, at this stage of our love, considering our mental and physical handicaps, I don't think we can perform it well, and we'll end up pretending. In either case, it's going to be traumatic. I brought pills for us, but I'm afraid they could kill us."

"How?"

"Your aneurysm and my hips bursting open during the excitement." With that, Lucy erupted into laughter again.

Dan muttered, "I don't mind going to heaven together."

Dan continued to explore Lucy's mind. "So where does this *semi-love* thing fit in our contemporary society, Professor?"

"It's common. Girls do it when they feel the guy is perfect and safe, not minding even getting pregnant and married."

"Like dreamy student nurses trying to entrap interns?"

"No way, Jose."

"You don't mind getting pregnant and marrying me, right?"

"Oh, sure, only if we were young again."

"But you're young in mind."

"All seniors in love are young in mind. You know the word *rejuvenated,* right?"

"You've researched this matter very well," Dan said. "Perhaps it's for your next scientific publication, eh? Is it about some bumps that face seniors in love?"

"Not really. I've spent endless hours dreaming of how best to indulge you on this cruise, and I have every intention of enjoying you as much as possible by kissing, cuddling, and using the pills, but..."

"But what? You seem to be struggling, like Hamlet—To Do or Not To Do!"

Lucy just chuckled.

After a long pause, Dan said, "It appears that sex is much easier said than done for seniors, just like when we were teens. Rather than dancing around it, perhaps we should get bombed like when we were in your apartment in Chicago and see what happens."

"I remember that night vividly, Dan." Lucy blushed. "We were totally stoned, yet we didn't have an accident, even though we slept cuddled tightly, completely naked. When we woke up, we were so scared we just dressed up in a hurry and went out for breakfast without saying a word. We looked around for the morality police and their spies."

Lucy and Dan had grown up in Korea when boys and girls were indoctrinated with Confucian teachings not to commit premarital sex. The morality police were everywhere to punish the sinners.

"I studied human anatomy and examined innumerable female patients," Dan said, "but when it came to you, you were a total mystery."

"How about now? My body is like a prune—dry and flabby."

"No, Lucy, you're still luscious and enticing. So I'm going to devour you very soon."

"Caveat emptor, Dr. Frankenstein. My flesh is still poisonous after swallowing a bitter pill when you ditched me. Still, even with age we can make our flesh appealing if we spike some love potions."

"What kind?"

"Blue and pink pills."

Dan concluded that Lucy was a Lorelei and that he should tread gingerly. Soon Dan screamed, "Oh, Lucy! I need a cold shower, stat!" *Stat* was hospital lingo meaning *right away.*

"Oh no," Lucy protested. "Don't you ever leave me all alone again. Never. Forget the shower for now. We'll do it together later."

Dan found that the mere mention of a cold shower deflated their bodies.

Lucy also noticed and grinned. "A cold shower could be the treatment of choice for priapism." She was referring to the most serious side effect of the blue pills.

They both fell asleep in each other's arms.

When Dan awoke, he was happy to see Lucy in his arms. When she opened her eyes, Dan said, "I didn't know you also had quite a few surgeries."

Lucy was surprised. "What are you talking about, Dan?"

"You had your appendix and uterus out, and you had a couple of hernia repairs and few minor breast surgeries."

Lucy was livid. "You bastard. You examined me

without my permission? You're a dangerous guy to sleep with, Dr. Frankenstein. But I also had three C-Sections and ovaries out."

"As a retired specialist, I couldn't help but go all over a beautiful naked lady in my arms. But you won't find my fingerprints anywhere."

"Then how did you exam me?"

"My snout."

"What? You sneaky weirdo."

At that moment, realizing it was noon already, Lucy reminded Dan that they should have put up Do Not Disturb sign outside their door.

"I did that when I went to bathroom earlier."

Lucy quipped, "Thanks to your prostate."

Dan started pillow talk. "With my huge aneurysm and recent heart attack, most likely I'll die first. Being a frugal grandma, I don't think you'll waste even a drop of your tears on me when I die."

"No. It's not that I don't love you but because I spent them all on Charlie."

"Will you come to my funeral, Lucy?"

"No. Again, it's not that I don't love you, but you'll be buried next to Linda, and I have to honor Linda because she was my alter ego."

"If you die first, I shouldn't come to your funeral either, right?"

"No. Again, it's not that I wouldn't like it, but it'd be like your coming to my wedding to Charlie. You'd be an inconvenient distraction." Seeing Dan in a daze, Lucy said,

"The funeral is for our eternal journey together, as we had promised."

"Then are we *secret* semi-lovers?"

"No, transient and occasional."

That made Dan cry, "Oh my. Modern-day senior romance is very complicated."

"It could get messy and nasty, so we have to be careful."

After a long pause, Dan asked, "You said transient? Isn't a love always forever? Eternal?"

"Our love is eternal so it has resurrected, and will go on and on forever. But our love in this segment in our senior years is going to be short, Dan."

Dan was pensive for a minute. "Senior romance is definitely not for procreation. So, sex can be deleted."

"Yes. As you know, love is a God-given birthright, and for young people that is primarily for procreation but not for seniors." When Dan seemed confused, Lucy said, "In fact, senior love is an aberration, but it's a special privilege given only to those few who linger on, while the vast majority of surviving seniors suffer from broken hearts before quickly passing away to join their deceased mates."

After a long minute, Lucy cried out, "I am a terrific kisser! So are you. So don't delete the kissing and cuddling from our senior romance. Otherwise, it would be too bare, too sterile."

"Add love potions and a cold shower and everything in slow motion."

Sometime later, Dan asked, "If you die first, can I visit your tomb?"

Lucy nodded. "I don't see why not."

"Thanks. Then I'll be visiting you and my old friend Charlie together."

"We both will be happy to greet you, Dan."

"You can visit my tomb, if I die first, and say hello to Linda as well. Our cemetery is near the airport. Our plot has a bench-type marker."

"Bench-type? Not a pyramid to fit your ego?"

"No, Lucy, I cannot afford that. Anyway, the plot is so small there is no extra room to hang around. So you can fly in and drive by if you are in hurry, or in bad weather; otherwise, sit on the bench, thinking about me." Soon Dan asked, "Would you like to visit Linda's tomb next week?"

"Yes, I would. And you should visit Charlie's when you come up to Chicago."

Lucy then said she was hungry, and Dan said, "We've been busy cuddling all day and missed breakfast and lunch altogether."

"It's the best way to lose weight on the Love Boat."

The next day, Dan woke up first. Lucy was still in deep sleep, so he went to the gym alone and watched a beautiful sunrise while pedaling an exercise bike. Later, they had a leisurely breakfast and went to the upper deck to watch the peaceful ocean passing by.

At lunch, the cafeteria was busy. Four thousand Love Boat guests had nothing much to do but eat. After a few bites, Dan said, "Yesterday you talked about lovers and companions when you lectured me on *semi-lovers*. It sounded like your ideas were based on Sir Francis Bacon, although he didn't mention semi-lovers—but I could be wrong."

"Who? Francis Bacon? Oh, that great British

philosopher, author, scientist and statesman? No, Dan. What I said was my own thought, but I could have been influenced by Bacon, as we all had to study his essays. But what's the issue?"

"I was so curious how this *semi-lover* thing would fit into Sir Francis Bacon's maxim that I went to ship's internet café on my way to gym and made a copy."

He pulled a sheet of paper from his back pocket and said, "As you know, I'm referring to his essay *'Of Marriage and Single Life'*—'Wives are young men's mistresses, companions for the middle age, and old men's nurses,' but there's no semi-lover anywhere in his essay."

"I don't think he ever mentioned it, but let me take a look, please." She was studying the paper intently, so Dan went to get more food.

Soon Lucy was in full *professor* mode. "This has been popular and much has been studied around the world over the centuries. I'm not a literature major, so I could be wrong, but I think the line you're obsessed with is about the chaste women, meaning good women. They serve their husbands well as mistresses, companions, and nurses when young, middle-aged, and old, but in my opinion, it needs to be updated." Seeing Dan puzzled, Lucy said, "For one, it is male chauvinistic. It was perfect at the time it was written, but now that gays and lesbians can legally marry, the word *wives* could be changed to *mates*."

"What about the single life?"

"His essay was about the young folks. The singles he referred to were those young unmarried people. He did not address much on nursing care or elders and nothing on divorce or widows or widowers, although they're the byproducts of marriage."

"Interesting observation, Professor."

"Again, I could be wrong, but senior romance was not on his radar, and I wonder what he'd say about it if he were in this century. He might add on to his essay, but more likely he'd write new essays on seniors' plights—demanding nursing care, grieving, and falling in love in old age."

After a long pause, Lucy said, "All married seniors eventually lose their mates, many of them after bearing herculean nursing tasks for a long time, just like you and I did. Everyone grieves, and while still grieving, some of them fall in love, and a few of them remarry, while some others become companions and mistresses the second time around, even without getting remarried—all in old age." Lucy finished with a huge sigh.

"Perhaps senior romance is a new social phenomenon as people now live longer. Perhaps even in Bacon's time, seniors in love were outcasts and ostracized and brought great anxiety and shame to families, so he skipped mentioning it altogether."

"I don't have the slightest idea how to answer that question," said Lucy.

"When we were in college, all we talked about was the mistresses and companions, nothing on nursing care. It's the same in the contemporary comments and debates on the internet. Even later we didn't know the magnitude of nursing care required in old age. Nonetheless, we didn't want to burden each other or our children with nursing, so we bought nursing home insurance. But when Linda had her stroke, I was compelled to care for her at home until she needed more-advanced care. But I'll use it sooner now that I'm alone, but I won't stay there too long. They will make a fortune from my policy."

"Why do you say that?"

"My aneurysm will finish me quickly, so I might never use my insurance, even after paying premiums for three decades. Although they say the average nursing home stay is two years, I might not stay that long. People just die when they get there. Patients lose their will to live, and overall being in a nursing home shortens your life."

"You sound like a lawyer."

Lucy wondered aloud how those married but childless people Sir Francis Bacon mentioned would fare in old age. "I think they'd suffer a great deal more than we have when a mate dies. My grandkids keep me alert, occupied, and happy. Otherwise, I'd be six feet under already. When single people get old, the good thing is that they don't have any obligation to nurse anyone, but then there's no one to depend on when they get sick. So they need assisted living and nursing homes."

After a long pause, Lucy said, "We need a new Francis Bacon for a new era."

"Professor Lucy, why don't you invent one?"

"Oh, no way, Jose."

It was the day for their first formal dinner. As dinnertime approached, Lucy tried on six different outfits in front of the full-length mirror. She paraded and twirled around like a fashion model. She looked dazzling, but she still tried a few more and finally settled on the ninth.

Now she was after Dan to dress up properly and chose

a white shirt and red tie. Dan felt the same pressure as if Linda was with him. It was definitely nagging more than a slight female touch, but that's what he'd missed so much. He concluded that nagging was an essential part of intimate companionship, the same as in marriage.

They took the elevator down to the dining hall. It was jam-packed with all the formally dressed people, young and old, unlike in daytime, when they were in cruising mode, all in casual outfits, many exposing pot bellies, warts, tattoos, and all.

All four couples at their dinner table were singles in their sixties and seventies. A retired sheriff and a retired nurse were from Utah. Two women couples were friends living together in Arizona. Dan thought they were more than friends. It seemed that more single seniors were openly cohabitating, not to mention sharing staterooms here. That made Lucy and Dan more relaxed. Marital status seemed to be a nonissue to these seniors. It was the Love Boat for everyone—single and married, young and old, gay and straight.

Dinner was average but the conversation was exciting, covering diverse subjects from diverse unmarried senior couples.

That night as they were about to retire, Dan whispered to Lucy, "Yesterday you said I needed a cold shower before going to bed, and on another occasion you said we both should take it together."

"Yes, but what else is on your mind?"

Dan knew Lucy could read his brain waves and would

answer even before he finished his question. "Then we should do it together from tonight," Dan said haltingly.

"That's a terrific idea! It won't be too different from sitting together in the hot tub, as long as we both cover those unsavory things."

Dan silently thanked her for being on the same wavelength. "Why don't I wear a *fundoshi*, and you wear your usual chastity belt?" A fundoshi was a Japanese loincloth, similar to those a sumo wrestler wears.

"That's another terrific idea from Bashful," Lucy said.

When Lucy squeezed into the shower to join Dan, she was wearing only a bright-red thong, while Dan was wearing swimming trunk. With a big smile, Dan muttered: "If I ever survive this water-torture chamber, I'll need hot sake."

"Don't have a heart attack, Dan. I can't do CPR in here. But I'll share your sake!"

In Cozumel, they briefly ventured out to the pier areas, both of them using their walking sticks, and bought souvenirs for their grandkids. This was where the two women couples from their dinner table were going to see the Mayan ruins, but Lucy and Dan ruled out any long land tours because of their limited locomotion.

From the beginning, Dan wanted to snorkel, but Lucy was against it. Later, though, she changed her mind, and they had a great time in Cozumel.

On the fourth night, while watching TV, Dan absentmindedly asked Lucy, "Whatever happened to our blue and pink pills?"

"They are locked up in safe. But we can't use them because something else happened," Lucy said matter-of-factly. When he pressed her on it, she said, "TSA confiscated my toothpaste and surgical lubricant because terrorists can bring plastic explosives in those large tubes, like the shoe bomber."

"So that's why you've been using my toothpaste. TSA has become the morality police."

"They were a little paranoid, I think," Lucy said sheepishly.

Dan pretended to be upset. "So does this complicate our consummation?"

"Not really. I prefer our million-dollar nap for the time being, considering all the complications."

"What complications? Like pregnancy?"

"Duh, be quiet. Otherwise, I might get a miracle cruise quintuplets. The complication will be mental, sending us to hell. It will be worse than falling off the deck and fighting with a shark for my life with my bare teeth."

"Teeth vs. teeth? Lucky that you still have your teeth."

Soon Dan smiled. "Don't you worry, Lucy. We can't waste those precious commodities on our honeymoon. We have to improvise, and we can."

"How?"

"Among the few options, plan B is simply buying the real lubricant from the general store on deck five, and in case they don't have it, or we're too shy to go there, plan C would be okay too."

"What's plan C?"

"Butter."

"What? Butter? What's butter got to do with it?" Lucy asked skeptically.

"I read about it in a novel by Alice Munro, the Canadian Nobel laureate in literature."

"I've read some of her stories too, but I don't remember any butter story," Lucy said.

"I don't remember the exact title, but it was definitely in one of her forty-plus stories."

Lucy was now interested. "So what's it about?" When Dan explained it in detail, Lucy just moaned. "I don't believe it. It's gross. We're not going to use it."

"Oh no. Butter is clean, safe, and even edible. It's a ubiquitous home remedy in Canada. They use it on burns, shingles, rashes, and even on sore joints."

"Is that all you learned while in Canada?" Lucy barked.

Dan countered, "As a certified bookworm, you are supposed to believe everything written in books."

"Oh, sure. You believe all the news on TV, right? Fake or not?"

"But you have to trust Nobel Prize–winning stories. Butter worked so well, perhaps that's why they gave her the prize."

"For butter? Oh, forget about it. We will stick to our million-dollar nap," said Lucy, shaking her head.

While soaking up subtropical sun at poolside, Lucy teased Dan when a buxom girl in a bikini ambled by: "How do you feel when you see such a pretty girl as her, you old monk?"

"Not much. Beautiful girls remind me of my

granddaughters. How about you? Do handsome guys attract you like when you were young?"

"No, my grandsons are far more exciting to watch than any others. But aren't you attracted to old ladies? They look rich and charming, the perfect sugar grandmas."

"Yes, but I don't think I could handle them."

"You mean in bed? With pink pills they could be lethal to someone like you—fainthearted." Lucy smirked.

"Not only that but I'm weary of nursing."

"Nursing?" Lucy asked with wide eyes.

"Yes. First of all, I'm burned out and can't nurse anyone anymore."

"I think putting up some nursing is a nice quid pro quo for having a good time."

That evening they dined at the buffet area while looking at the brilliant sunset. They went to the upper deck and sat poolside. It was breezy. Holding hands, they watched an old movie on a huge screen. Some kids were eating ice cream, so they had some too. The night was romantic.

The next day, they arrived in Jamaica, where it was very hot but breezy. They explored only the immediate pier area. Lucy lamented, "Too bad we can't explore the shore. It sucks to get old."

Lucy remembered to buy souvenirs for her grandkids. She and Dan fell asleep after a late lunch—she on the bed, he on the sofa.

It was another formal dinner that night. Lucy tried five different dresses. The dinner mates were now familiar with each other and had a wider range of topics, including their shore excursion stories. They had a good time. After dinner, Lucy and Dan strolled through the ship's downtown. After a drink, they went to the top deck and watched a movie on the big screen while eating popcorn, like when they were young.

That night Dan whispered to Lucy with a wide grin, "I got it. The real lubricant."

"What? Where did you get it, Dan?"

"When I went to gym, I happened to meet the sheriff, our dinner-table partner, and after I told him about the TSA saga, he made a special trip back to his stateroom to get an extra tube of lubricant and three blue pills. He said these are special personal gifts to you from his companion—a fellow retired nurse."

"Seniors are engaged in illicit trades on the Love Boat! I wonder what else goes on under the table."

Ignoring her, Dan said, "He also said blue and pink pills are God-sent boons for seniors, and the lubricant is the best-selling item on all Love Boats."

Lucy retorted immediately, "Forget about it, Dan. I lost interest in pills after your butter story."

Dan feigned surprise. "Oh no! It was TSA, not Alice Munro." Dan said the sheriff was going to write a letter to the TSA chief on the wisdom of confiscating surgical lubricants from traveling nurses, "I can imagine your expression when those young TSA guys took the things away from a shy grandma. I hope you didn't lose your composure."

"Definitely. I didn't want to make a scene for such a minor thing."

"Minor? It's a major thing for any honeymooners, quasi or not. You should have put up a gallant fight, throwing your handbag at them."

Lucy smiled meekly, and soon confiscated the goodies and locked them up in the safe.

On their last evening, Dan surprised Lucy. "Hey, darling, I have a dying wish."

"What is it?"

"We should enjoy a great finale of our honeymoon cruise with a big bang."

"How?" Lucy was curious.

"At the farewell dinner, we'll have all the proper rituals, with intimate song and dance, champagne, and..."

"And *what*?" Lucy yelled out.

"Get bombed and crash, like in Chicago, but after taking pills together."

"No way, Dan. I'll dance and drink, and I might even get intoxicated, but I prefer our million-dollar nap."

As expected, disembarking was long and tedious, but the bus ride to the airport was shorter. At the airport, the boarding process was not complicated, as they were now more careful, and the flight home was uneventful.

Dan bought a bouquet of yellow roses at the airport gift shop before going to Linda's grave. "Are yellow roses Linda's favorite?" Lucy asked. "They're my favorite too."

As they sat on the bench marker at the cemetery, Dan saw Lucy's eyes cloud over. They were silent during the whole time they sat there.

CHAPTER 8
After the Cruise

ONCE THEY WERE HOME, THEY had a glass of red wine, toasting to their nice companionship on an uneventful cruise, their second time of getting together. They were tired and soon went to sleep in the master bedroom. They were now comfortable sleeping together, without a resurgence of guilt complexes. Rather, Dan felt he could not sleep without Lucy.

Early the next morning, Dan could tell Lucy was uneasy. She obviously was anxious to go home and probably was tired of traveling. Even more likely, she missed her grandchildren.

After one week with Lucy, Dan could understand her much better. Even after a half century in America, Lucy still retained her Korean kimchi temperament, as volatile as an Irish cabbage temper. She also showed arrogance every now and then that he had seen before. He thought that was from her super-affluent family background, but now she displayed an air of authority, justifiable considering her hard-earned credentials—a PhD and having been a professor, not a small feat for a small fish transplanted to a huge pond.

Otherwise, she was warm, humble, and vivacious and was basically a happy person, just like the original Juliet. By the end of their cruise, he found their chemistry compatible and their biologic rhythms synchronized, and they functioned well as nice companions for a week in the real world.

Over breakfast the next morning, Dan asked, "Lucy, did you enjoy the cruise?"

"Yes. It's good that we're back to our old puppy love, but taking showers together was the best."

"I liked it so much that I want to go on another cruise soon."

"To take a cold shower?" They laughed.

Lucy said this cruise was quite different from earlier ones she'd taken. With so many physical limitations, seniors like them could not exploit all the things the cruise offered.

Dan remarked, "We didn't even get much of a suntan because we spent more time cuddling."

Lucy added, "The shower stall was so small it was like when we were in the Adirondacks." On that trip, a sudden snowstorm had forced them to crawl into a single sleeping bag. Lucy finished their story. "In the morning, we were very proud of having saved each other from freezing to death. Then we were able to rent a cabin and enjoyed sleeping together for the next two nights."

"But you were wearing that chastity belt," Dan said with a sigh.

"Not true. You were a born loser. I wanted a baby, but

you wanted to save everything for the official honeymoon and acted like a Buddha statue." The term *Buddha statue* was popular Korean vernacular when they were young, referring to a lifeless person. Lucy continued. "Had we made a baby, our fate could have been quite different, living in an igloo village, happily ever after—ice fishing and hunting caribou for a living, rather than chasing illusive research grants."

"That's how my second book, *Under the Northern Lights*, begins. We have a wonderful life," said Dan, sighing.

"*We?*"

"Sorry. *They*," Dan quickly corrected himself.

"I haven't read your books but will soon."

That evening, they decided to use the hot tub. After a while, Lucy said, "I am so hot I am going to take everything off. Is that okay?"

"Yes. Too bad that you still have hot flashes. We have complete privacy. The previous owner was a middle-aged single woman. She said she never wore a swimsuit in this tub."

"Okay. From now on, I shall skinny-dip."

After that, Lucy always skinny-dipped whenever she came to Denver. To Dan, Lucy was an adventurous grandmother, young in mind. Or maybe it was that all seniors in love behaved like teenagers, all rejuvenated and reinvigorated.

The next day they woke up at almost the same time. Lucy said, "I feel the house is moving, rocking gently, just like the ship."

When Lucy started to get up, Dan pulled her down and

whispered into her ear. "I want pillow talk. My brain works better if you hold me tight."

"You're beginning to like it. Caveat emptor, Dr. Snail: It's habit-forming."

"You mean I may have to move in with you?"

"No way, Jose. But what's in your mind, you old monk?"

"What's the statute of limitations, Lucy?"

"In what? Are you worried about some malpractice?"

"No, I never was sued while in practice. My question is when a widow or widower can fall in love with impunity."

"Impunity?"

"Yes, without being hated by family, friends, churches, and society."

"You're probably confusing it with *mourning period*, when people are supposed to behave and avoid finger pointing and gossiping. Once you're over that period, people tend to accept the second marriage, especially for younger generations, but they don't like it for seniors at all. People think senior romance is a bizarre psychotic behavior, and it's the same with senior friendship and companionship, although a tad less. In the old country, the official mourning period was three years, but each person might have a different grieving period. Children mourn their parents' deaths for life, and they resent it when their surviving parent remarries. But in my opinion, the worst enemy is self-pity, just like with us."

"Is self-pity part of the mourning process?"

"Yes, the worst part."

"Back in old country, villagers still wear hemp ribbons for three years. It's from Confucianism, rather than from Buddhism."

"Hemp?"

"Yes, the pot thing, you know. Koreans also have harvested it for a long time for the fibers and made ropes, paper, and clothes." When Lucy seemed oblivious, Dan said, "Even in cities, they used heavy hemp tarps and cloths to wrap the remains and make funeral garments, hoods, and the ribbons."

"Those yellowish, stiff, tall hoods? Why would they use hemp products?" asked Lucy, surprised.

"Hemp cloths and tarps are sturdy and last longer in that environment six-feet deep, so they became traditional funereal material, I guess."

"Did they smoke it too?"

"The contemporary Koreans shun it, more from its close association with corpses, deaths and funeral services, rather than being illegal. A few smoke it anyway, knowing it's illegal, just like people anywhere, and some people use the leaves as herbs."

That was when Lucy exclaimed, "So cannabis is to Koreans what butter is to Canadians."

"Oh no, Lucy. As you know, it's ginseng that's just like Grandma's chicken soup in America." Ginseng was a popular herb in Korea for its anti-aging and cure-all beliefs.

After a long minute, Lucy said, "Have you tried it, Dan?"

"Hemp? Oh yes, when I was a research fellow in San Francisco, it was the epicenter of the hippie culture, but I could not inhale. I helped medical marijuana research when I was in private practice. That was for chemo-induced nausea. My patients claimed the government-issued pot was better than the street versions. You seem to be interested. Would you like to try it? In Colorado it's perfectly legal now. I voted for it mainly for decriminalization of minor offenses."

"Yes, I want to see the shops and try a joint. It's just out of curiosity for a new culture, good or bad," Lucy said calmly.

"I don't have any in my house at this moment, but I'll get some for you, and we'll visit the shop. It's an incentive for you to visit me again. It's a tourist attraction, they say."

Soon Lucy said, "Dan, we got side-tracked. Why did you ask me about the statute of limitations?"

Dan went blank for a moment. "Oh yes. A friend of mine had trouble. After losing his wife to a five-year battle with colon cancer, he had a huge funeral service, attended by the entire Korean community in his city. But in two months, he invited them all to a humongous wedding reception when he remarried. Rumors were rampant that his two children left him forever. It happened right here in America."

"How old were the children?"

"The boy was a freshman and the girl was a junior in college."

"I think their age was a big factor. They were still at a tender age to lose their mother, only then to see their father 'betray' their mother."

"I think one year is too soon, and ten years might be too long, but what about three years?" Dan asked.

Lucy was confused. "What are you babbling about?"

Shaking his head, Dan said, "It's been three years for both of us, but we don't want to lose our kids or grandkids."

"That's one sure thing. They cannot be collateral

damage. Some say they resent the mothers more than fathers when a parent takes in a stranger. Kids are more attached to Mom than to Dad, beyond the Oedipus complex, you know."

"Yes. We both will have to stick to our Eleventh Regret."

"What the heck is it, Dan?"

Dan cleared his throat and then proclaimed proudly, "Do the best for your children and grandchildren; otherwise you'll regret it when—"

"Did you invent it or plagiarize it?"

"What? Plagiarize it?" "Yes, God already engraved it in our genes—X chromosomes, the genes for motherhood. That's reason why all the mothers across the animal kingdom fight to the death to feed and protect their babies."

"I thought I was brilliant."

Soon, Lucy said, "After three years of a hard single life, you deserve a mistress to cook for you."

It took Dan a minute before he said, "Ha-ha. I don't think Sir Francis Bacon said mistresses should cook; everyone knows wives have to cook."

"Any live-in mistress will cook for you while acting as a wife."

"I don't need anyone to cook meals because I'm a certified master chef, thanks to you."

"Thanks to me?"

"Yes, after you banished me to Canada, I had to endure the single life for three more years, and I had no choice but to become a master chef—self-taught."

"Self-taught?"

"Yes, I made spam soup first and then Korean instant noodles when they became widely available."

"Oh my."

"But I'll cook for you if you move in, as my live-in-mistress."

"No way, Jose. I hate instant noodles!"

That's when Dan solemnly swore, "When I cannot cook noodle soup, cannot drive, cannot dress myself, or I become leaky, that's when I'll surrender myself to a nursing home rather than taking in a mistress."

"No mistress will bite your bait then, not even with a million bucks."

Soon Dan lamented, "So our senior romance has lots of limitations and disincentives: we cannot procreate, cannot attend the other's funeral, and cannot be buried next to each other. What else have we agreed on, Professor?"

"We're not to adopt each other's children or grandchildren. Also, we are not going to move in with each other. We need physical space between us. Also, when one of us dies, the other should fade away, quickly and quietly."

"Fade away?"

"Yes, before becoming an inconvenience or an unnecessary distraction to the other's family. I want my kids and grandkids to remember only nice things about me, nothing bad at all. I think that's enough for us for now. Don't you get any other smart ideas!"

"Quite complicated. So that's our quasi prenuptial, eh?"

"No, Dan, those are the basic ground rules for our senior romance."

"More complicated than our puppy love rules."

"Not really, but one more thing, Dan. Although we love each other, we cannot give or take anything tangible from each other."

"Not a dime?"

"Companionship is the only thing we can share for now; it's precious but intangible... like rainbows."

"Rainbows?"

"Yes, they are precious but intangible, transient, and ephemeral." Seeing Dan in a daze, Lucy added, "I mean, you cannot possess them, and they're sweet but short."

After a long silence, Dan said, "I have one last question. Do you want our semi-love secret or open?"

"We can't hide it from our own families or close friends, but we don't want to advertise it to the whole world. So how about *semiopen*?"

"Semi-legit semi-lovers going semiopen? So what's the top priority of our senior romance, Professor? It's obviously not for procreation."

Lucy calmly uttered, "Our top priority should be relishing our intimate companionship as much as possible because we just don't know how long we will have it. Time is the most precious commodity to seniors, yet they don't appreciate it, let alone enjoy it."

At the airport, waiting for Lucy's flight back home, Lucy said, "I had a great time with you at sea and also in bed. I am going to miss you terribly. It's been a great diversion from the grieving. I hate to leave, but we will get together soon."

CHAPTER 9
Chicago Visit

AFTER THE CRUISE, DAN FELT as if he was waking up from a long hibernation or rising up after being buried for a long time. He now had some sense of purpose and direction in life.

He found himself thinking about Lucy all the time and hoping to see her again soon, so one day Dan called her with a suggestion. "I miss you so much I'd like to visit you."

"I miss you, too. When can you come?"

Dan was happy. "Soon, but only if it's okay with you and your kids."

"Why my kids?"

"We've talked about this before, Lucy. We have to watch their feelings carefully. We don't want to alienate them at any cost."

Lucy agreed. "Let me think about it, Dan."

She called Dan the following week. "I think next week would be perfect for me and my kids. My son is back from his out-of-town conference. Everyone is in a happy mood."

"Okay, then. I'll make reservations for a hotel and a car."

"Why don't you stay with me?" Lucy was surprised.

"Thanks for the invitation, but I think I'd better stay in a hotel this time. It'll look politically correct."

Lucy was quiet for a moment but said, "I think you're right. Yes, politically correct."

Moments later, Dan said, "I want you to take me to an opera or the theater while I'm there."

"I don't know what's playing. You used to like *La Bohème*, I remember."

"Aha. Your memory is coming back nicely. It doesn't matter what we see as long as you sit next to me."

Later, Lucy wanted to read Dan's current love story, so he emailed his latest manuscript.

Dan checked into the Palmer House in downtown Chicago. He wanted to get reacquainted with the Loop as well because that was where they used to hang out in their younger days.

Dan went to Lucy's home first. It was a nice and big house. He could visualize all the kids and grandkids filling the house, but in between, the house was much too large for an elderly woman living alone.

Lucy took Dan to a Korean restaurant not too far away, where her family was waiting. Besides Lucy's two children and their spouses, there were five grandkids. Lucy introduced Dan as a family friend, her husband's med school friend, who also went to grad school with her.

Dan tried to recall all the grandchildren's names but couldn't remember anyone but Julie, the youngest.

The family was a happy and lively bunch. They entertained themselves, and no one asked Dan any questions. It was easy for Dan for now, but he knew everyone was watching him closely. As the dinner was ending, the youngest daughter, Iris, asked, "So you guys went on a cruise together? Was it fun?"

"It was a nice diversion," said Dan.

Julie jumped in. "Can I go on a cruise with you next time, Nana?"

"Yes." Lucy smiled.

"Promise?" Julie asked.

"Yes, dear."

Julie was happy now.

Back home, Lucy showed Charlie's study to Dan. It had bookshelves on two walls that were full of medical books, along with professional memorabilia—diplomas, certificates, and awards that both of them had accumulated.

In one corner were neatly stacked copies of the *New England Journal of Medicine*, the most prestigious weekly medical journal, to which Charlie had subscribed for life, now suspended in time.

On another wall were Charlie's portrait and their wedding pictures. Dan looked at them for a long time. He also saw Lucy and Charlie in many family pictures, spanning over their lifetime together. There Dan saw Lucy in various stages of her past—a skinny, ambitious grad student with shoulder-length hair that he was familiar with; a happy young mother with short hair; a well-coifed, self-confident middle-aged professor; and the present graceful grandmother.

Dan said, "I can see your lifetime events in a single,

panoramic view, like in a dream... like in a movie. They are the events that bypassed me."

Lucy agreed. "I wanted to see the same in your room, but they were all deleted."

He sat down in Charlie's chair. There was a monitor on the desk and an old computer terminal underneath. "So this is Charlie's shrine. He was a real lucky guy."

"You could have been in Charlie's place, Dan."

"I don't think so. Charlie was the perfect guy for you."

Lucy just blushed.

"I feel Charlie's presence," he told Lucy, who was now leaning on the desk next to him.

"I feel the same. Whenever I have a problem, I sit down here and talk to him."

It was clear that Lucy was dwelling on Charlie's ghost, and she would never let him go.

Back in the living room, Dan asked her, "How did I do today?"

"You did okay."

"I hope I didn't hurt their feelings."

"So far, so good, but you never know."

"You have a beautiful family. I could see Charlie's DNA imprints on each and every one of your offspring. Your DNA was more dominant in your daughter and granddaughters; they're very pretty, like you."

Lucy blushed and said, "They all have Charlie's personality."

Dan saw a picture of a little girl playing violin. "Aha. Some of your grandkids play violins."

"Yes, two of them. They get private lessons. How about yours?"

"One was getting private lessons, but she quit. Another is with Suzuki. Do you still play violin, Lucy?"

"Oh no, my fingers, you know. I gave my violin to my oldest granddaughter. How about you? You miss playing cello?"

"No. The only thing I can do now is listen, and I don't know how long I'll be able to do that."

Lucy felt nostalgic. "Remember what a good time we had playing duets, especially *Solveig's Song?* But our next-door neighbors always yelled at us for making such horrendous squeaking noises."

"While I languished in Canada, I used to cry whenever I heard even a part of it, thinking about you and our golden days in Chicago."

"Same with me too."

That was when Dan told her about seeing double rainbows while listening to Solveig's Song on the car radio, just before receiving Lucy's request to be a Facebook friend.

"I sent them together to reach out to you, Dan."

The next day when Lucy came to the Palmer House to pick up Dan for the opera, she screamed. "You're now an obscene bloody bourgeoisie bastard, staying in an opulent hotel."

"No, Lucy, I just wanted to impress you and pretend to be a sugar grandpa, but obviously it backfired. I confess the YMCA is still my favorite—the poor man's Hilton."

Making a face, Lucy said, "Oh, sure. I believe you, Dan. When you came to see me last time, you stayed at a downtown YMCA after coming all the way from Canada by bus."

"How did you know?"

"Paul told me everything... just before he left town after getting his PhD." Paul was their mutual friend in their graduate student circle. He was now retired in Texas, but Dan had not heard from him for a decade.

"I had a strange premonition that you might be getting married soon, so I hoped to see you one last time, but Paul told me you were already married. He didn't tell me the details, nor did I ask him who the lucky guy was. I knew everything was my fault. I knew you'd be happy. I didn't want to bother you, and I was resigned to my fate." Dan said he visited few places they used to hang around before going back to Canada.

A few minutes later, Lucy asked, "Did you see any opera then?"

"No, I was too emotional. It could have driven me to self-destruction mode."

"Glad that you didn't go to homicidal mode."

The only opera they could see was *The Merry Widow*. They watched it while holding hands.

"This middle-aged widow is very happy, unlike older widows like us," Lucy observed. When Dan seemed baffled, Lucy said, "She will become a mistress and companion the second time around... merrily, while she's still young."

At the intermission, Dan looked unhappy, and Lucy said, "Sorry. We should have seen a sad opera to suit your mood."

"No, Lucy. I'm crying because I'm so happy to be with you, just like the olden days."

"Are you sure?"

"Yes, I still see sad operas whenever I want to cry for two to three hours nonstop. It's the same for comedy shows when I want to laugh for a few hours uninhibited."

"That could be quite therapeutic for a semi-cuckoo like you, suffering from Pseudobulbar Affect," quipped Lucy. She then explained that Pseudobulbar Affect was a psychiatric disorder that caused uncontrollable laughing and crying spells.

"Yes, better and cheaper than seeing a psychiatrist," said Dan with his head down.

The next day Lucy took Dan to Charlie's grave with a bouquet of yellow roses. Lucy saw Dan in deep thought and heard him mutter, "Oh, Charlie. You lucky guy. You stole Lucy from me, but thanks for taking such good care of her."

The following morning Lucy called. "I need a cold shower in your hotel, Dan."

Dan was surprised, "What? Did you run out of cold water in your home?"

"Oh, be quiet. I also need to exercise at the swimming pool there and would like to go over your manuscript. I'll bring my laptop."

After swimming, they used the hot tub together. There, Lucy said, "I miss skinny-dipping."

In his room, they took a shower together before going to bed to "relax". They were playful, the same as on the cruise ship. Later, they opened their laptops and went over a few things Lucy wanted to show Dan, while sipping red wine that Dan had ordered from room service. It was truly a nice working session in a relaxed atmosphere.

After thanking Lucy, Dan smirked. "Semi-lovers in a semisecret tryst."

"Yes. And we are procreating something that is purely intellectual. Your book *Near Miss* will be our miracle baby."

They ordered room service for lunch, rather than going out. They worked on and off with few *rest periods*.

At around three o'clock, as she was leaving to meet with a granddaughter to go shopping, Lucy said, "I think we need a few more sessions on our project." When Dan was too slow to catch her meaning, she declared, "Dan, you're going to stay here for one week. I'll be reporting to work in the morning. We'll start with swimming, okay?"

At the door, Lucy said, "Your book is basically finished, so you don't need my help except in a few areas and proofreading. You could finish it in a month if you do the homework I give you each day."

CHAPTER 10
Old Faithful

ONE DAY IN LATE MAY, Dan asked Lucy if she would be interested in going on a camping trip.

"Oh yes. The cruise was our quasi honeymoon and a great diversion. Where are we going?" Lucy was eager to get together again.

"I'm thinking Yellowstone, but my ideas are not fixed."

"Yellowstone sounds great."

"I'm thinking mid-June before it gets too congested. Later, there'll be more tourists than all the wild animals combined."

Lucy was excited. "How are we going there?"

"I tow a small travel trailer, about eighteen feet."

"Is it easy to tow?"

"Yes, you guys pulled U-Hauls when your kids went to college, right?"

"Yes, quite a few times, but that was a long time ago, and Charlie wouldn't let me drive."

"I traded my larger trailer for this smaller one after my heart attack so that I could handle it alone."

"What does inside look like? It must look like a mobile Hilton."

"Huh. It's basically a mobile YMCA, with a toilet and a shower on wheels," Dan explained.

"Is that it? Can we still take a cold shower there?"

That surprised Dan. "Um, huh. Yes, but one at a time, not both of us together."

"Why not?"

"Two excited people at the very end of a tiny trailer could tip it over, either backward or sideways."

"Oh no." When Dan said it also had a microwave, a gas grill, two bunk beds, and a living room area that converted to a bedroom, Lucy said, "Now it does sound like a Hilton. This is exciting. Is your trailer big enough for two adults to slumber?"

"Yes, up to four grown-ups. We also can pitch a tent outside, but not in Yellowstone because of known bear attacks. Again, everyone will say that we slept together under one roof, but if anyone asks for the details, say that I slept on top of you, while you slept in the lower bunk bed."

"How big is the bunk bed?"

"About the size of a coffin."

"Coffin? Sleeping in a coffin will be a new experience, let alone seducing you there, eh?"

"In a coffin?" They both laughed. "I am glad that you're coming. I'll make a campsite reservation there. The Grand Canyon isn't too far from there, but we probably can't get a reservation, although I could try."

"Perhaps we could go there next year," Lucy suggested.

"Yes, but I can't plan anything beyond six months."

"Aneurysms suck," Lucy blurted out.

"What's so special about Yellowstone?"

"Watching hundreds of geysers and wildlife. Although it offers many outdoor activities like fishing and hiking, it's usually drive-by events for average seniors like us," said Dan.

Lucy called a week later. "What do I have to bring, Dan?"

"Not much but the usual spring outdoor outfits, but also bring one heavy winter inner wear and a swimsuit."

"Then it's for all four seasons."

"Yes. The mountains can get cold at night. Also, it could snow anytime at that high altitude."

"Oh, like the Adirondacks?"

"Yes, you can use Linda's boots and winter jacket because you're about her size."

"You trashed all your memorabilia but saved Linda's things?" Lucy asked in surprise.

"Yes, dear, just few. Our granddaughters are getting taller, so I have saved some of her clothes."

The morning after Lucy came to Denver, Dan brought his trailer home from its storage facility. After looking at it inside and out, Lucy said, "It is bigger and better equipped than I was expecting."

When they were making a grocery list for the trip, Dan said most of the camping foods were essentially "bachelor food."

"Bachelor food? What's that?"

"Canned and dried foodstuffs that bachelors live on, especially single seniors like me."

Lucy smirked. "I'll cook a few simple things for you."

"That'll be a great upgrade. Then I'll treat you to my specialty thing," Dan said with a big smile.

"What's that, Dan?"

"Korean instant noodles."

"I'd rather eat bear steak rare!" Lucy said with mock anger.

That evening Dan took Lucy to a nearby Mexican restaurant to meet his family. She was very entertaining, and Dan saw that his grandchildren had a good time with her.

His home was south of Denver, so they started early to cross Denver's downtown area before rush hour. They stopped one hour later at a truck stop.

"I'll drive for the next two hours, but in Wyoming, I want you to test drive when the traffic is light."

Lucy nodded. "I can do that."

After a break at a restaurant at another truck stop, Dan asked, "Do you feel like test driving?" When she nodded, Dan started his instructions. "As in anything, you adjust the mirrors, seat, and so on. You handle the trailer just like your blind old monk—gingerly and in slow motion. Turning has to be wide."

"Huh. Slow motion? I might fall asleep on every turn." Once in the driver's seat, she panicked. "I can't see the back in the rearview mirror."

"Sorry. I forgot to tell you. This trailer doesn't have a rearview camera. So we have to use two outside mirrors only and imagine what's behind us."

"Huh. It's just like you, the blind old monk."

The truck-stop parking area was huge. She started like a new learner, first with stop and go. After circling the parking area twice, she said, "Okay, I think I'm ready for roadkill," and she headed out onto the interstate. There was no traffic when she entered the freeway. As she gained confidence, she practiced driving at various speeds and changing lanes.

Soon she said, "I like it. Thanks, Dan."

"You're a quick learner, Lucy."

She drove for another hour. Dan brought out two cowboy hats from a compartment in the trailer. Putting a smaller one on Lucy's head, he said, "Perfect. It was Linda's. I'm glad I didn't trash it."

"You've been traveling with Linda's ghost."

They took a few selfies with the RV in the background and also with Lucy in control, all in cowboy hats.

"You're now a certified retired urban university professor, driving an RV in the Wild West."

"This is a completely new experience," Lucy said excitedly.

The road to Thermopolis, Wyoming, was narrow, but Lucy handled it very nicely. After checking into a motel, they went to a hot springs center.

"The hot springs are as popular in America as in Korea."

"Why is that?" Lucy asked.

"It has a healing power. It has a high sulfur content along with many other minerals. They say it's good for skin conditions, arthritis, and many other ailments, including heart troubles."

That's when Lucy said, "Better than Canadian butter?" They both laughed.

Dan said the residents there received their hot water

from the city, all geothermal. They ate at a fast-food place. They were tired, so they retired early.

After passing Cody, Wyoming, Lucy drove the trailer all the way to the eastern entrance of Yellowstone National Park.

"You're our wagon master," Dan said, "now entering Yellowstone."

Lucy was excited: "I need a six-shooter and a Winchester!"

"Yes, Calamity Jane!" He was referring to a heroine in old western movie that was popular when they were young.

The campsites were jam-packed. "It's like Times Square," Lucy observed.

Soon they explored the downtown and went to the bridge area. There were huge crowds waiting for the buffalo run. Soon the herd came and passed by an inch from Lucy. She screamed, but she liked it and took up-close pictures of a drooling buffalo.

The next day they toured all over Yellowstone. The Old Faithful geyser was crowded.

Dan said, "We are two 'old faithfuls,' Lucy. We got together after forty-five years. So if we ever get separated, we should meet again right here in exactly forty-five years."

"We should meet sooner, like every other year. Perhaps we could come back in other life forms, like butterflies."

"Oh no, that's too soon. After we die, we both will be with our mates."

"Oh, shoot. You're right. Then we should meet right here again in forty-five years."

"Promise?"

"Yes, my dear Old Faithful," said Lucy, holding him tight.

The next day, they drove down to the Grand Tetons.

Lucy said, "Majestic, Dan. But it's déjà vu. I've definitely seen this before, perhaps in my previous life."

Dan agreed, "Yes, you were a charming Indian princess, Lucy. Don't you remember? When you were in deep trouble, Alan Ladd came to rescue you."

"Alan Ladd?"

"Yes, he was a darling cowboy in the old western movie *Shane*."

"*Shane*? Ah, that's it. I saw it at least ten times when I was young. We all tried to learn English from American movies. But I don't remember seeing the lake."

"That's because they deleted the lake."

"Deleted the lake? Can they do that?" Lucy was skeptical.

"They edit movies, as you know. They filmed the movie in nearby Jackson Hole with the Tetons in the background without showing the lake."

"Oh, my heavens. How did you know?"

"It's on Wikipedia, the internet encyclopedia."

In Jackson, they saw a sidewalk arch made with elk horns. It was unique. Dan told Lucy that local Boy Scouts collected elk horns to sell to Asian merchants.

"Ah, those famous American aphrodisiacs are piled up on the sidewalk, unguarded?"

Dan nodded. "Yes, you're in paradise, Lucy. The streets

are paved with gold bricks, with just a few potholes and scattered horse dung."

They went to a restaurant. Dan said, "They don't have bear steaks today on the menu, rare or otherwise, but how about elk steak?"

"What do they look like?"

"Like that one, Lucy," he said, pointing a mounted elk head on the wall.

"It looks so gorgeous. I cannot eat his flesh."

"How about a venison burger?"

"That one?" she asked, pointing to a deer head mounted on another wall. "Wow. I'll sit out from all the local delicacies and go vegetarian from this moment." She ordered eggplant.

The next day she was sick with nausea. She said she also had pain in on the upper right side of her abdomen but felt better after vomiting.

"It could be morning sickness," said Dan.

"Holding your hands only?"

"It could be pseudocyesis, false pregnancy with the same symptoms."

"No way, Jose."

"Could be food poisoning?"

"I don't think so, Dan. I ate everything well cooked. You and I shared practically everything, and you're not sick."

"But I have a totally different stomach, Lucy. While attending the Seoul University of Hard Knocks, I lived on famine food. So I'm immune to food poisoning. What about the bacon and ham?"

"What about them?"

"They are all fat. We ate ham sandwiches yesterday. Do you have fat intolerance?"

"No," Lucy answered but stopped their conversations there.

That evening they dined at Jackson Lodge. Lucy ordered local trout. She did not have an upset stomach. The view of the Tetons and the lake that evening was mesmerizing, even eerie, with a full moon shining.

On the way home at the end of their trip, they decided to visit national parks in Utah and headed south. Lucy was now the de facto wagon master, literally in charge of driving and its care, including kicking tires on each refueling stop. That was one good thing for old Dan, but she was also a terrific back-seat driver who would tell Dan what to do almost every other minute.

When Dan complained, she said, "You're a horrible, senile driver, making me very nervous. Among all the things, you drive too slowly, many times way below the minimum speed limit, Dr. Snail."

She talked to one of her seven grandkids nonstop when she was not back-seat driving. She bought souvenirs whenever possible. It was obvious that she was enjoying the road trip immensely.

When they were setting up camp near Arches National Park, it rained hard, but the storm system moved eastward. Soon they saw double rainbows rising above Arches at a distance. Lucy put one arm around Dan's waist and started humming Solveig's Song. Dan joined her. Their eyes filled with tears.

"Beautiful double rainbows pop up suddenly but fade away soon without leaving a trace. Sweet but too short," Lucy lamented.

When they toured Arches the next day, Dan exclaimed, "With this much moisture, desert flowers will blossom in a few days."

"Are they ephemeral also, like rainbows?"

"Yes, ma'am. Scorching desert heat reduces them to nothing, but they keep coming back whenever conditions are right, and the life cycle is renewed."

"Like our puppy love? It's back and thriving, even in our waning years, but we just don't know how long it'll last."

On the way back, Dan said, "Good to have a sexy companion."

"Oh, shut up, my shy strange-bedfellow."

"Shy? Neutered?"

"Yes, but don't count on me for nursing you. I'm allergic to nursing."

"Oh my. A retired nursing professor hates nursing after putting up so much nursing care on her dying mate. I'll get young buxom chick instead."

"Good luck, Dan. As soon as those bimbos get what they want, you'll be rotting in a urine-smelling nursing home, penniless."

"Huh. I hated the stench whenever I made nursing-home rounds, even in the expensive private nursing homes. That's the worst fear I have about nursing homes, more than beefy orderlies."

"Everyone hates to go to nursing homes, more than going to hell," Lucy agreed.

After driving for a couple of hours, Lucy asked, "Dan, why are you so quiet?"

"I was busy looking at you... your beautiful profile."

"Oh, you dirty old monk. You aren't blind at all. You still don't have cataracts. Do you remember reading 'Of Travel'? That was another essay by Sir Francis Bacon."

"Yes, but what's the point, Professor?"

"Of all things, he said people traveling on land usually don't write much, even though they see so much, while sea travelers write quite a bit, even though they see nothing but the sky and sea."

"Yes, I remember."

"You were quite talkative at sea, but now on land, you're too quiet. Too spooky, Dan."

"Sorry, Sir Francis's principles don't apply to me at all."

"How come?"

"Whenever I am with you, I go nuts because you're so sexy...whether at sea or on land."

"Oh shut up, you old monk."

Some moment later, Lucy asked, "Dan, how is your love story going?"

"I'm in a mental block. I need your help, like a week or two in Chicago or in Denver."

"Oh, you miss a cold shower? I miss it too."

The morning after arriving home, Dan asked, "So do you really want to visit the shop?" When Lucy did not understand, he said, "The hemp shop."

"Oh, yes!" Lucy was excited.

Dan said Denver had more hemp shops than Starbucks. They went to Dan's favorite place downtown. It was not crowded, but they saw a few seniors. Lucy was very observant and had a long chat with a saleswoman. She bought an ointment for her hip, while Dan bought few joints and his favorite candies.

Later, Dan asked Lucy, "So what did you think of the shop?"

"Not much different from tobacco shops and liquor stores. They checked IDs and probably had surveillance cameras. The senior customers definitely didn't look like aging hippies."

Obviously, it was anticlimactic after much anticipation. Dan said the pot was popular with some seniors, like beer soon after Prohibition, when some states allowed alcoholic beverages while others did not.

Back at Dan's house, Lucy tried a joint in the kitchen, but she could not inhale deeply. She stopped after trying only half of a joint. Later Dan helped Lucy put ointment on her hips. She said it was anti-inflammatory and wouldn't affect her brain. She was already an educated consumer. Later that night, she tried Dan's candy but did not feel any effect.

That's when Dan said, "It works for me. One small candy puts me to sleep."

"Aha, it works as a placebo."

The next morning when she woke up, Lucy complained of headache.

Dan asked, "How bad is it?"

"Bad enough to complain to you. It used to be just once in a while, but lately it's been happening more often and more intense."

"Have you seen a neurologist?"

"No, but I will."

"Would you like to go to ER here? They can give you a brain MRI."

"No, I think I'll be all right. I'll take a few Advil for now," she said, but she stayed in bed.

Chapter 11
Surgery

ONE DAY LUCY SURPRISED DAN with her news. "I'm going to have gallbladder surgery next week."

"Oh my. What's wrong with your gallbladder?"

"I have gallstones." Lucy explained that after the Yellowstone trip, the vomiting continued on and off. An ultrasound test showed multiple gallstones, but her primary physician insisted that her symptoms were not from gallstones because the pain was mild, if there was any. He said 25 percent of seniors had so-called "silent gallstones" and Medicare would not allow the surgery unless there was significant pain.

Lucy wanted to see a surgeon, but instead she was sent to a gastroenterologist for an upper endoscopy. On the day of the procedure, the physician canceled it, saying that a second endoscopy in just one year wouldn't be too much different. Finally, Lucy was sent to a surgeon, Dr. Sohn, who recommended immediate surgery.

Dan asked, "Your son Peter agreed to that?"

"Yes, dear. They both said it should be taken out as soon as possible before causing any damage."

"Who's going to nurse you?"

"My children and their spouses will take turns."

"They're all busy people. Can I come to take care of you? Or at least give you a hand?"

Lucy was silent for a minute before she said, "You're too old and too inexperienced."

"No, I took care of Linda through umpteen surgeries, including gallbladder surgery two years before she passed away."

"But that was when you were healthier and more alert. I should be up and around in just few days."

"Yes. Still, someone should be with you around the clock, and it'll be easy for me, even with my back problem. Regardless, I want to be there."

"Let me talk to my kids first. Okay?"

The next day Lucy called. "My daughter and daughter-in-law were going to take turns, but they said you're more than welcome."

"Thank you and thank your kids."

"We'll arrange things that way," she said.

Dan was excited. "You don't mind my staying at your home for that long?"

"No, Dan."

"If I stay too long, we'll start quarreling because we both have loose tongues."

Lucy chuckled, "That'll be fun, too." Lucy obviously was pleased.

The next day Lucy said, "I'll pick you up at the airport."

"No, I'm driving."

"It's over a thousand miles. The way you drive, it might take ten days to get here."

"With my adrenaline gushing already, I might get speeding tickets for a change. I also want to make a quick trip to my old town in Ohio."

"You can use my car for that."

"I'd rather use up my jalopy as much as possible before putting it to sleep."

"Your car is not that old."

"Yes, it's my old faithful, but it's like me, having seen better days. It's going to be my last car."

"Why do you have to go to your old town? Do you still have mistresses?"

"Yes, all in the cemetery. But you know I lived there for forty years, and Ohio State is another place I want to visit. My youngest went there, and I have to make a final round. They also have at least ten Korean restaurants in the city, and I have to visit one of them before I die."

"Okay, then. I have no further questions. I know it's all because of that aneurysm." When Dan was silent, she said, "But in the airplane you said you had nothing you longed to see, eat, smoke, or drink."

"The same holds true, Lucy. I've done that with Columbus already, but as long as I'm there, I'd like to make another quick round."

"What Korean dish could be your dying wish? Is it bulgogi?" Bulgogi was Korean barbecue.

"No, it's oxtail soup."

"Oh my."

Driving dawn to dusk, the trip took Dan two days. Lucy gave him the guest room, which was on the main floor, the same as the master bedroom that had been Charlie's sick room. She had intercoms in several rooms.

Lucy gave Dan a tour of the house. He'd been there before so it was not entirely new, but he paid special attention to the kitchen, bathrooms, and the medicine cabinet. Dan asked, "Do you have laxatives?"

"Yes, they are here."

"Do you have a Fleet enema?"

"No."

When Lucy seemed to be skeptical, Dan said seriously, "You might need it later. Linda needed it on about the third day after her gallbladder surgery." When Lucy pouted, Dan said, "I'll get couple of them from the supermarket and return them if you don't use them."

Later, he asked Lucy to take him to her supermarket. "Beside Fleets, I want to pick up some bachelor food."

"What is it, Dan? You told me about it before, but I forget. It has to be an exotic bird food for an eccentric blind old monk."

"Ha-ha. It's *food for thought*." Then he reminded her it was instant noodles and spam for a lazy old bachelor.

"Oh my heavens. You've been subsisting on junk food. We should put you in assisted living as soon as my gallbladder is out."

The next day many family members and friends visited Lucy. Dan stayed in his room most of time, but he met her doctor son, Peter, and her daughter Iris. When Peter and Dan were alone, Peter said, "Thanks to you, our mom is almost back to normal."

"What did I do to your mom?"

"She quit gambling soon after meeting you on the way to Korea."

"Gambling?" Dan was surprised.

"Yes, Dr. Dan. She got deep into poker games soon after our dad passed away."

"I didn't know about that. With her high IQ, she probably was beating everyone, but I cannot imagine her wearing a poker face."

Peter asked Dan about his medical problems. "I could set up an appointment with a world famous heart surgeon in Chicago. He's well known for mini-procedures, including aneurysm and valve repair at the same time."

"Thanks for your offer, but I'm happy with my surgeon. I'm an old man, waiting for my time to go."

On the day of the surgery, Dan took Lucy to the Ambulatory Surgical Center at the hospital. About one hour after she went into surgery, Dan was startled when Dr. Sohn tapped his shoulder from behind. He whispered in Dan's ear, "Lucy did well. She had lots of stones."

Before Dan could stand up, Dr. Sohn was gone. Dan had several serious questions, but he realized that Dr. Sohn had told him all the information he needed in ten seconds—that everything went well.

Sometime later he was called in to the recovery room. Lucy was dopey but looked fine otherwise. He texted Iris and Peter: "Your Mom is in recovery, doing well." Coming home was smooth. This brought some old memories of Linda when she had the same kind of surgery. When they arrived home, Dan again texted Iris and Peter to let them know she was home and doing well.

Lucy slept through most of that afternoon. Later, she needed help going to bathroom. Dan gave her medication regularly. She ate chicken soup for supper, which she had prepared before the surgery. Iris came and stayed for two hours. Later, Peter stayed three hours. Lucy went to bed early. That night Dan slept on a sleeping bag on the floor in the far corner of the master bedroom, waking up whenever Lucy made a noise.

On the second day Lucy was more active. She did well, and nothing special happened. Only a few of her immediate family members visited her. Others called, and Lucy handled all the calls herself. On the third morning Lucy decided to take sponge bath. Initially, she said she could do it alone, but soon she asked Dan to rub her back. When he'd almost finished, Lucy cracked, "A retired physician is giving a bath to a retired nurse."

"No, I'm sticking to your advanced version of Sir Francis Bacon's maxim—a *semi-lover* giving a tender loving bath to his semi-lover." That extracted a smile from Lucy.

That evening all five of her grandkids visited her.

Late afternoon on the third day, Lucy said she was constipated, but she managed to pass a bowel movement. Dan gave her another laxative tablet. The next morning around seven o'clock, the intercom squeaked, and Dan heard Lucy call out, "Dan! I need you—stat!"

When he rushed to her room, she was rolling on the floor.

"What's going on? Are you in pain?"

"No. Constipated, I think... damn it!"

"Let me check your belly. Turn on your back, please."

Poking Lucy's stomach here and there, Dan asked, "Where is your stethoscope?"

Between moaning and groaning, Lucy said her grandkids had damaged hers, and Charlie's was locked up in his desk drawer upstairs.

"Then let me listen to you the old-fashioned way." He knelt down next to her, putting his right ear to her belly. "You have normal bowel sounds."

"Lucky that you don't wear hearing aids."

Dan ignored her and said seriously, "With a soft belly and normal bowel sounds, there is no obstruction. I think you're right—it's impacted. I'll have to remove some digitally."

"Digitally?"

"Yes, dear, with fingers, not with a plunger. Could I check?" When she nodded, he asked where the surgical gloves and lubricants were. She pointed under the sink for the gloves but said she did not have jelly. Dan immediately responded, "That's the one the TSA confiscated? And they followed you all the way home to seize the rest of them. You have Vaseline, right? I've seen it somewhere." He found it in the medicine cabinet.

After some work was done, Dan said. "I think the Fleet enema will do a better job from this point, Professor."

"Then use it."

"Yes, ma'am."

It took a long time before Lucy said she had to go to the bathroom. Dan helped her to bathroom. Sometime later, she came out, looking pale. He helped her to bed.

"You've been stoic and haven't used pain pills too often,

but even that much caused this much trouble. Any pain now, Lucy?"

"Yes... but only on my pride."

Later, he said, "I was going to use butter if you didn't have Vaseline."

Lucy was aghast. "Butter? Oh, here we go again. That Nobel Prize–winning Canadian secret formula. I haven't touched it in months."

On the fifth day she was almost back to normal. After lunch she said she needed a rest. Instead of going to her bedroom, she walked to Dan's room and lay down on his bed. She soon pulled him down until they were looking at the ceiling. Touching Dan's face, she said, "I miss a cold shower."

"How about recuperating in Denver for a week or two? We could go to the nearby hot springs and hold peace treaty talks."

"With hemp incense, hot mineral baths, ginseng tea, and my chicken soup, I'll recover in no time."

By Saturday. Lucy was much better. At around eleven that morning, Iris came to relieve Dan of official nursing duty. They sat down at a coffee table, and as Dan handed over medication sheets, he said, "Everything seems to be going well, but she still needs narcotics occasionally and should take stool softeners on a regular basis for a few more days."

"Thank you very much, Dr. Dan. You are a good nurse."

"Oh, a good nurse's aide. Your mom is a nursing professor but a perfect model patient and extremely nice to her caregiver."

"You saved me from going to the ER," Lucy said, smiling. "I give you an A-plus."

"For the enema? I was only a Good Samaritan as a board-certified specialist in enemas."

They all laughed. As Dan was leaving, Iris said, "Thanks, Dr. Dan. It's so far from your home..."

She made him feel welcome and appreciated, instead of rejected and regarded with suspicion.

Dan headed straight east on I-80, and checked into a Holiday Inn in his old town east of Cleveland. The next morning after driving by his old lakefront home, old office, and two hospitals, he headed south to Columbus and visited the dorms and then his favorite restaurant.

At home, Dan texted: "Hope all is well."

Lucy texted back: "Doing better. We all appreciated your excellent nursing. Semi-lovers also need good nursing mates. Closed a couple of nostalgic chapters?"

Dan texted back: "Yes to Columbus but not to oxtail soup—not yet."

One month later, Lucy flew to Denver. They took a short camping trip to Mount Rushmore with a stop in a hot springs resort on the way home.

After this trip, they visited each other every six to eight weeks, avoiding holidays and all their grandkids' birthdays.

CHAPTER 12
Balloon Festival

IN EARLY SEPTEMBER, DAN CALLED. "Hey, Lucy, I got a great idea for our fall camping trip."

She was excited. "Where could that be? I am already interested. I really enjoyed Yellowstone and Mount Rushmore. The fresh air was good, as well as being away from the same old grieving and urban chaos."

"Have you heard about the biggest balloon festival in America, perhaps in the whole world?"

"No, I haven't. Tell me about it."

"It's in Albuquerque, New Mexico, at the beginning of each October."

"Are you going there in that rickety porta potty, or by car?"

"Both. My jalopy will pull that tattered buggy—and add two confused seniors."

"A pathetic foursome. Should I bring anything special?"

"You could use a sweater," said Dan.

When Lucy called a week later, Dan said all the campsites and hotel rooms were already completely booked around Albuquerque, and the only campsite he could get was one with no sewer hookup.

"Can we still take cold showers?" Lucy asked, concerned.

"Yes, dear, but only if we drain the waste water often. They have a dumping station and shower facility, but we have to drive our car each time we use it."

"It's going to be an experience," said Lucy.

"The good news is that we have three nights in Santa Fe with full hookup. On the last day there I have to winterize the camper before coming home."

"Winterize?"

"Just before storing it for the long harsh winter, I have to put some antifreeze solutions here and there to prevent the pipes from freezing."

"What about Santa Fe?" Lucy was curious.

"It's an old western city, rich in history and the arts. You'll like it."

Lucy flew in. On her first evening in Denver, they had dinner at a restaurant with his family. Dan noted that his grandkids were now good friends with Lucy, although his kids still were reserved. Dan thought more frequent interaction with her would lessen their anxiety.

As before, Lucy—in a cowboy hat—was in charge of their trip. The road was mostly flat through the foothills of the Rocky Mountains until they reached the New Mexico border. From there it was high desert with mesas but much easier than driving to Yellowstone.

On their first day they went to the balloon festival site at five thirty in the morning. It was still dark, but the main tent city was already bustling. A group of eight balloons, called the Dawn Patrol, took off, floating away one after another, with impressive light shows. Later in the morning, there were balloon rides, but they skipped that because of their limited mobility. Lucy said, "Aging sucks."

They came home in midmorning because there was nothing much going on. The balloon festival events were all held predawn to midmorning. They explored the city in the afternoon.

In the evening, Lucy complained of a headache.

"I should take you to the ER. It's not too far," Dan said.

"I'll be all right. I'll take a couple of Tylenols."

"Are you sure?"

"Yes, Dan."

"I think you need an MRI."

"I'd need preauthorization for that."

"No, you don't need a referral in an emergency."

"I'll see my primary first."

"No, Lucy, see your son Peter first because primary guys work for HMOs, not for you."

Mass Ascension was the main event for the next day. As dawn broke, balloons near and far began to shape up. Crews worked hard, and they all seemed to be family members and friends. Gradually, the balloons started to go up. By nine thirty, the entire sky was filled with balloons of various sizes, from dots between the clouds to gigantic balloons ready to go up in the next field. Many were shaped to please kids and grown-ups alike—spider, pig, cow, chicken, elephant, and cartoon characters.

Dan and Lucy sent pictures to their kids and grandkids. Their response was great.

Their campground in Santa Fe was a nice place with full hookup. They wanted to visit one of the Indian cliff-dwelling sites in the area but decided not to go after learning that it involved a stiff uphill walk and also climbing a ladder. Again, Lucy muttered, "Aging sucks."

The next day they went to the historic downtown and took a bus tour. That afternoon they toured the city themselves, and enjoyed evening time around a campfire.

On the third morning, when Lucy came back from the supermarket few miles down the road, Dan called out, "We have to get out of here—fast!"

"What's wrong?"

"There was a family of mice... inside the trailer!"

"What?"

Dan said he saw an ugly baby mouse first, then three other babies, and then a beautiful mother mouse. "I pushed them out, and now they're gone. I checked all over. I'm sure there isn't any mouse inside, but I don't want to sleep here tonight."

"No way, man." Lucy agreed.

"I need to winterize the camper before we go to a motel," said Dan and asked her to stay in their car but she insisted on learning about it.

"All right. Then you'll need to wear boots, a mask, and surgical gloves, to protect yourself from possible mouse attack and droppings."

They finished the winterization in one hour but did not see any mouse or droppings in the process. On the way to a motel, they bought quite a few mousetraps and poisons and placed them strategically inside the camper.

"Mice in the bed!" Lucy screamed in the middle of night, jumping out of the bed.

Dan got up fast, grabbed the bedcover from the bed, and started to shake it.

Lucy stood next to the bed, bewildered. "What are you doing, Dan?"

"You said there were mice in the bed. I want to kill them all."

Lucy helped him shake the bedcover, blankets, pillows, and pillowcases one by one, but they could not find a mouse anywhere, not even under the bed. Finally, they gave up.

After half an hour, they were back in bed but could not sleep. Dan asked, "Are you sure you saw mice?"

"No, I didn't, but I felt them."

"Where?"

"In your feet area," said Lucy, touching his toes.

"I didn't feel anything." Then he said, "Ha. You scared the hell out of me, Lucy."

"What's so funny?"

"You could have touched my toes and thought they were mice."

They were wide-awake for a long time, just staring at the ceiling without saying a word. Suddenly, Lucy broke silence. "Do you know how pestilence is spread?"

"Pestilence?"

"Yes, the Black Death thing---also known as pest and plague."

"Aha. You are trying to scare me the second time around. It strikes the southwestern United States once in a while. I heard two people died last year right here."

"Oh my God. What do we do?"

"Nothing for now. I think the babies were just born, and the mother mouse looked healthy, and they didn't bite me. No fleas bit me either."

"They still could carry the germs. We'll be all right for the next ten days, but beyond that, we'll be sweating and praying to God."

"Ten days?"

"I could be wrong, but the incubation period might be about that long, and we could die soon after."

"Want to go to ER?"

When they were on a straight valley highway, Dan thought Lucy looked down in the dumps. When he asked her what was going on, Lucy said she finally had read Dan's second book.

"The story sounded real," she said. "Obviously, the main character is you, but Mia, the girl you fall in love with, seems like me. The setting is different but everything seems like when we were in Chicago. At the end, you guys elope to Canada, only because Mia was carrying your baby."

"It's obviously fiction, Lucy—those *'could have been'* things, you know," Dan blurted out after a long silence.

Ignoring him, Lucy said, "I have an advice for you. I don't like the sad ending of your current manuscript. It's heartbreaking to see this girl, Amy, kicking and screaming, pleading to go to Canada with you, but you refuse. It's just like what happened to me." Lucy was in tears.

On the first day in Denver, they went to a hemp shop and bought a few goodies. The shop was crowded, and again there were several seniors. Later, Dan asked Lucy,

"Do I look like an aging Asian hippie? You know I come here once in a while."

"Oh yes, one with his brain riddled with HIV."

Later that afternoon, Lucy wanted to visit a local casino, so Dan took Lucy to Linda's favorite place, fifty miles deep in the mountains. The casino was packed with seniors; a few of them came with canes, while others were in wheelchairs. Some were wearing oxygen cannulas and carrying portable oxygen tanks. From the road signs along the way, Lucy knew the elevation was 8,300 feet.

"The air is very thin here, almost a mile and a half above sea level," Lucy said. "They need higher oxygen doses or hyperbaric chambers, rather than just a 'no smoking' room."

Dan echoed, "Oh, a pressurized casino, like the one that they'll build on the moon?"

Soon Dan cried out, "It looks like payday."

"Payday?"

"Yes, the day when seniors receive their monthly Social Security checks. That's the day when they swarm the casinos like locusts. Nursing homes send them by the busloads. Casinos give them multiple coupons, including free meals and even cash."

Most of the seniors were busy on the slot machines. Unlike old days, slot machines were no longer one-armed bandits. They responded to fingertips and did not make jingling sounds, but there were the seniors' loud, hoarse roars whenever someone hit the jackpot.

When Lucy joined a blackjack table, Dan studied her face, rather than her hands. He saw that she smiled all the time instead of having a poker face, even when bluffing. He realized why Lucy's family was so concerned. Lucy could have been a "senior addict," just like other seniors in the casino that evening who burned away their monthly Social Security checks and even some of their retirement savings.

CHAPTER 13
New CT Scan

WHEN DAN HAD ANOTHER ECHOCARDIOGRAM, he reported the results to Lucy. "After a year, the aneurysm has grown to 5 centimeters from 4.8, and the aortic stenosis also is worse—"

"Please speak slowly, Dan," she interrupted.

"It's worse, Lucy!" Dan blurted out in disgust.

"Those are just numbers. I don't think you have any symptoms of aortic stenosis," she said, surprising him. It was clear that Lucy was keeping an eye on him. "As far as the aneurysm is concerned, you'll need a CT scan."

"Thanks, Lucy. My surgeon said he also does mini-surgery, repairing the aneurysm and the heart valve at the same time, with a minimal incision, as Peter mentioned, but only if my heart is okay by cardiac catheterization."

"The *mini* still means a sizable cut, and it's still a major intervention for an old man, no matter what they say. My guess is that you'll need another echo in six months to check the valve status."

Dan thanked Lucy for comforting him with positive thinking.

That's when Lucy said, "Life is short, Dan. You should enjoy it as much as possible. You should find an oxtail soup place there, and eat it every week, if not every day."

Two weeks later, Dan called Lucy. "The surgeon called me with the new CT report."

"And?" Lucy was apprehensive.

"The aneurysm is the same at 4.8 cm."

"That's great news for you, Dan. Let's have a drink. I'll drink one whole bottle of red wine here today, cheering for you. You should drink one bottle there also. Promise?"

Lucy dreaded Dan's biennial heart tests as much as Dan did.

The following week Dan told Lucy he'd had a complete annual physical. The primary physician said his prostate was enlarged but refused to order a PSA test, a screening blood test for prostate cancer, saying that it was against Medicare rule on seniors older than seventy-five. Dan said he almost did it by self-paying but did not because he didn't want to know if he had prostate cancer; he already had enough problems on hand.

He also told Lucy that a month earlier, his primary physician refused to refer him for a five-year follow-up colonoscopy, in spite of Dan's history of multiple polyps, some of them premalignant. He said it was against Medicare rules. Dan's friend and neighbor had a similar situation with the same primary doctor. He simply switched to another primary to get a referral, and the test found two premalignant polyps. Dan did not want to change his primary, so he faked rectal bleeding, and the test found four polyps this time.

Lucy said, "We seniors definitely are a terrible burden to society. Medicare, HMOs, and our primary guys are banded together to dump us rather than fix us."

Two weeks later Lucy asked Dan to visit Chicago, saying that she had found a good oxtail soup restaurant there. "I also have a new Korean recipe from my sister," she told him.

Dan asked her again to help him with his manuscript, insisting that finishing his book was now more urgent. Lucy agreed, and Dan flew to Chicago the following week.

Dan checked into a hotel near Lucy's neighborhood. He still did not want to upset Lucy's children or grandkids by staying with her. He went to Lucy's home in the morning for breakfast with oxtail soup. It was delicious. They came to the hotel and went about their routine—swimming, hot tub, cold shower, "relaxation" and working on his manuscript. For lunch they ordered room service and went to the oxtail soup restaurant for dinner. There, Dan declared, "Your soup is better than this."

For the next three days, Dan ate breakfast and supper at Lucy's home, feasting on oxtail soup. At the end of his stay, Dan complained that he was five pounds heavier.

Lucy also complained. "What do I do with all the leftover ox-tails?"

After a long pause, Dan smiled. "Deep-freeze them for now, Lucy. I'll be back next month."

CHAPTER 14
San Diego

ONE DAY IN LATE APRIL, Lucy said she had to go to San Diego to babysit her middle child's two children while her daughter and son-in-law took a long-planned European trip.

"When are you going there?" Dan asked.

"Memorial Day weekend."

"Do you think I could visit you while you're there? My middle guy will spend that weekend in his Malibu condo, and I'm planning to visit there."

"You know I'll be busy with the two boys; they're seven and nine."

"I won't interfere with your job. After Malibu I could drive down to San Diego on your last two days. After your job is done, we could visit Philip and Helen together, and you could help me drive home... via Las Vegas, Sedona, and Santa Fe, and then fly out of Denver."

"Oh, the blind monk needs a professional long-distance chauffeur."

"I need a philosopher companion."

"Not a Xanthippe?"

"She's okay too because she made Socrates greater, so her nagging could be intellectually stimulating. I also want to meet your middle child and her family, if possible."

"You're not driving that rat-infested porta potty, are you, Dan?" Lucy asked, sounding as if she was shivering.

"Oh no. My trailer is too bulky for this type of trip. Also, you'll be anxious to get home too."

As usual, she said she'd think about it, and after a week, she said it was a good idea.

After checking into a hotel near Lucy, Dan visited her in midafternoon. She seemed to be doing well with the boys, Jason and Albert. They had homework to do, and she didn't need anything from the supermarket, so Dan went back to his hotel.

At around eight o'clock that evening, Lucy called Dan for urgent help. "I have to take Jason to the ER—he has high fever, but I hate to drag Albert along. I can't call the usual babysitter on such short notice."

When Dan arrived, Lucy explained calmly to Albert that she was taking Jason to see a doctor and that Dan would stay with him. She was home in two hours. She said Jason had a febrile virus disorder, and there was no new prescription. Jason was still feverish but not as much.

After putting Jason to bed, she checked on Albert, who was sleeping in his own bed. Dan volunteered to go to supermarket for liquid Tylenol and Gatorade. Lucy asked him to buy saltine crackers as well. Dan made a quick run to his hotel to get his laptop and a small overnight bag.

In a couple of hours, Dan realized Lucy was exhausted, so he urged her to take a nap, saying that he would watch the boys for the next few hours. She agreed to and set up a baby monitor before going to bed. Dan stayed in the living room with TV on but on mute mode. He checked on Jason whenever the monitor made a noise. Lucy woke up in two hours and checked the boys. Jason was not as hot and was in deep sleep, she said.

Lucy thanked Dan and told him to go to his hotel, saying that she now could handle the boys alone, but Dan asked her permission to stay on, just in case. When Lucy asked him to sleep in her bed, Dan said, "I'm back to my old habit of sleeping on the couch."

"Are you eating noodles and spam too?" she jibed.

Early next morning Lucy said Jason was cool, and she thanked Dan for staying overnight. After a leisurely breakfast, Lucy sent the older boy to school, but kept Jason home. She talked to Jason's pediatrician. Later, she put him on the couch to rest, with cartoons on the TV. When there seemed to be a lull, Dan urged Lucy to take shower and volunteered to do the dishes.

Around ten in the morning, Dan went to his hotel to shower and exercise. When he came back at around noon, Lucy was now in a full nurse's mode, checking Jason for fever and hydration and also feeding and entertaining him. When her daughter texted her from Italy, Lucy reported everything and said she hoped to send Jason to school the next day.

Dan stayed with Lucy all day. Lucy was in full grandmother mode when Albert came home. Although Jason was much better and his fever rose only slightly, Dan stayed that night, taking turns, just in case, but nothing much happened.

By the next morning Jason was much better. He ate well and was active. Lucy decided to send him to school. Later, Lucy called the school nurse to see how Jason was doing. In midmorning Dan went back to his hotel to shower and swim. Back at Lucy's, Dan worked on his laptop, while Lucy was busy cleaning house—her daughter was coming home the next day—and preparing dinner for the boys, but she sat next to Dan from time to time. For lunch they had a pizza delivered.

At around one o'clock, Lucy suddenly jumped up and rushed to her daughter's home office. A few minutes later, she shouted to Dan to come in. There, Dan saw Lucy sitting on floor, putting rosin on a violin bow. She said it was her daughter's. Pointing to a cello standing against a wall, she asked Dan to play it, saying that it was her son-in-law's. Without much thought, Dan grabbed the cello and asked, "What are we going to play?"

"Solveig's Song." She put a pair of music books on the stands and said, "They like it too—short and sweet."

Soon Dan realized that he could not play cello at all: "I was a perpetual novice, and I've been idle for a good dozen years."

"Do it, Dan. You know you can!" Lucy shouted at him, and she started to play.

Dan brought the cello and the book to Albert's room at the far side of the house and started to practice, but it was not easy. After much difficulty at the beginning, Dan was able to play some, and later he joined Lucy, who was now playing like a virtuoso. Dan could play only half of the time, at times just shadow-playing.

After playing half a dozen times together, they were now reasonable. When they finished, Lucy hugged Dan with tears in her eyes. "We're back to our olden days, Dan," said Lucy, without trying to wipe her tears. "Who cares if we messed up few notes? No one's going to bang on our door."

About noon next day, Lucy called Dan to say her daughter and son-in-law were home.

"Do you need a break?" Dan asked. "We could go to dinner."

She was agreeable.

Dan met Lucy's middle child, Sherry, and her husband, Larry. Sherry said they had a great time in Europe and thanked Dan. "I heard you're a good nurse, but you're a good babysitter also."

"Thanks. I was just an extra hand," Dan said, deeply moved by her warm appreciation.

Later that afternoon, Dan and Lucy went to a seafood restaurant in La Jolla. After dinner, Lucy drove up the Pacific Coast Highway and parked at a scenic viewing area. Many people were enjoying the spectacular Pacific sunset. There, she kissed Dan.

"It's like we're back in time," Dan said, "to Lake Shore Drive, watching the moonrise."

After the sun went down, Lucy drove back to the city, but instead of heading to her daughter's home, she went straight to Dan's hotel. Seeing Dan puzzled, she said, "I need a cold shower."

The following day, the Choys invited Lucy and Dan to their home. Helen and Philip didn't say it, but they were pleasantly surprised that Lucy and Dan were very intimate. Lucy confessed that they were old sweethearts in training, and that the fiftieth reunion pictures and Facebook had helped them reconnect after forty-five years. She thanked them for being the middlemen.

When Helen smirked, Lucy whispered to her, "Don't you worry, pal. We're just friends. But you'll be the first to know when we do it."

Later, they went to a Korean restaurant for dinner. Lucy and Helen had as much to catch up on, as did the boys. Dan was especially curious about other classmates in the area.

Having spent six years together during their two years in premed and four years in med school, the classmates had a strong esprit de corps, in spite of having been highly conceited and competitive. They were especially proud of having rioted together in 4/19, the Student Revolution, which was an uprising for the fledgling democracy, as well as sharing in many volunteer works for social justices during their tumultuous med school days.

Philip was in a happy mood, especially after a few glasses of *soju*, which was their college drink. Philip said there were five classmates in the area. Two of their classmates' widows were in town as well, as they had moved there to be with their children and grandchildren, and they were always included in the monthly golf outings and dinner meetings, as the widows were lifelong friends with the other wives.

Philip said some classmates' marital status was less than ideal. He reminded Dan that most of the guys married only after their graduation, half of them by arrangement.

Though they were scattered after their graduation, classmates always tried to get together whenever possible, and wives played a big role, not only in feeding them but also trying to match up many of those still single with eligible partners. In doing so, the first wives had formed a formidable sisterhood, and they became extremely territorial, fiercely guarding their being doctors' wives.

Whenever there was a divorce, the first wives sided with ex-wives, regardless of the claims, and they hated the second wives, but their public enemy number one was foreigners, especially those replacing their classmates' Korean wives. Their aversion for mixed marriage continued for a couple of decades until their own children started marrying non-Koreans. They also did not like mistresses coming to their meetings.

When Philip's group tried to invite the widows in their area to the fiftieth reunion, some of the first wives in other areas wanted to invite those divorced first wives as well, whether or not the second or third wives were coming. Sensing great multiple family feuds, the class leadership torpedoed the whole idea of inviting the first wives, whether widowed or divorced.

On the way home, Dan said, "The widows should have been invited because they've been good friends with us. But I don't think they will accept us as a couple in their meetings here or in our fifty-fifth reunion in three years. It's a Hawaiian cruise, and it's going to be our last reunion. We'll be ostracized... I don't think they care about those lonesome widowed classmates."

"Philip and Helen might be an exception, but it's same with Charlie's class also. I don't think the first wives of Charlie's class will accept you, even though I belong to them, and many of them know you. The class sent a pot of flowers to Charlie's funeral, followed by a flurry of condolence cards, emails, and some phone calls, but that fizzled down to none in just a month. That's the end of our long friendship through immigration, training, and practice. Widows and families are discarded like jalopies. Our nursing college reunion was the same. That's why I didn't go to our fiftieth reunion. Helen went with Philip, but I was a widow. None of the widows went to the reunion." Lucy sighed heavily. "It tells us that doomsday is coming soon to your medical school class that you guys once claimed to be avant-garde— civilized and glamorous. Doctors are not immune to aging. They cannot heal themselves. So it's a time to repent."

"No, Lucy. Many of us are so forgetful we won't know how or what to repent."

"You've gone too far."

Moments later, Lucy declared, "Let's go to the reunion regardless of what they say about us. You want to see your lifelong friends and those wives who are still friendly to you... for the last time. I know many of them and want to see them too... like Helen."

Dan nodded.

On the next day, when Dan came to get Lucy for their journey home, he witnessed a beautiful farewell scene between Lucy and her two charming grandsons. Dan had to respect Lucy's love and dedication as a grandmother.

As they were driving out of San Diego, Lucy suddenly wanted to see Dan's second child, Gilbert, as long as they were so near. She had met everyone in Dan's family but Gilbert and his family. Dan called Gilbert and asked him and his family to meet them halfway, in Korea Town in Los Angeles--- considering the infamous LA traffic.

While driving north, Lucy said, "So Gilbert retired at thirty-four, exactly the same age as when you started your practice?" "Yes. When he sold his company, he bought me a drink for telling him not to go to med school, but he started another business in a year when he was so bored of retirement at such a young age."

Lucy knew Dan had urged all his kids to go for an MBA instead of medical school because his rural solo practice had been traumatic. He enjoyed being a doctor but did not like the social and business sides of medicine—never-ending malpractice crises, emerging HMOs, and working like a slave while the quality of life was so poor.

Gilbert and his family were waiting in a restaurant in Korea Town. Lucy had a good time with them, especially the two grandkids. After dinner Gilbert and his wife invited Lucy and Dan to stay that night with them, but they decided to drive on.

While in Las Vegas for two days, they did not do anything special, as they had been through the allures of Las Vegas. Lucy did not gamble. They just relaxed in the hotel, "recuperating" from babysitting chores and making up for lost time—swimming, the hot tub, cold showers, and "resting". At night they went to shows.

While driving to Sedona, Arizona, Lucy said, "I want to see the Grand Canyon one more time as long as we're so near. I saw it once with my family, but I want to see it again with you."

They were able to get a room in the village and spent a

day touring the Grand Canyon. Then they went to Sedona. It was a beautiful place. After spending one night there, they headed for Santa Fe.

When they were on I-40 in New Mexico, the highway was straight, and driving was monotonous. Lucy was quiet, so Dan asked her what she thought of his newest manuscript. He had emailed it to her earlier.

Lucy said, "I liked the happy ending. Thanks for that."

"But you are grumpy, Lucy."

She did not respond to that, but she muttered, "I finally finished your first book, *A Color Blind.*"

It was about a medical resident and a nurse in San Francisco, both from Korea. At the beginning, being a typically shy Korean girl, Suzy could not tell if the sunset over the Golden Gate was beautiful, so the boy called her *color blind.* Later, she got Americanized before the boy did and demanded a circumcision be performed before their wedding. In the old country, circumcision was rarely done at birth, but when done later, boys felt mutilated.

"Thank you for reading the book. How was it?"

Instead of answering, Lucy calmly demanded, "Who were the real target audiences of your books?"

"I had no one in particular, Lucy. When I was blind with grief, I found solace in writing."

"No way, Jose. Tell me the truth."

It took sometime before Dan admitted, "My grandkids. They are too young to listen to my stories now, but by the time they are grown up, I'll be dead. So I wanted to leave digital footprints for them."

"Oh, c'mon, Dan. That's a total hogwash."

It took another minute before he said, "I wanted them to know that their grandpa was an immigrant from a faraway country, funny-looking, and hardly spoke English at the beginning. He had to work hard like a slave, but he was a human being with feelings, just like any other American."

"That's holy bullshit, Dan. Too cliché. Do you really expect them to read all those adult things---kissing and all?"

That shocked Dan. "Um, uh. Not the stories in the books, per se..."

"Who then?" When Dan did not answer, Lucy blurted out, "You are a hopeless total jerk. As I told you some time ago, it was about us, without a doubt—you and me, to be specific. You stole everything from me." When Dan seemed dumbstruck, she yelled, "Suzy in the first book is me, and so is Mia in your second book, just like Amy in *Near Miss* now, in character and background. Much of the dialogue in all three are direct, verbatim quotes, stolen from me, when we were dating." After a long pause, she said, "You portrayed me as a naive, stubborn, uninitiated, old, ugly virgin, not once but in all three books. I'm going to sue you for libel, plagiarism, and also claim half the royalty."

"Suit yourself, and good luck. My royalties from those two books were near zero. I didn't put up any marketing effort, as I was just eager to publish the books with minimal expense."

Lucy yelled, "Why did you write such horrible stories about me, eh?"

"It's all fiction, Lucy."

"Oh, c'mon, Dan. That's a baloney, pure and simple."

When pressured more, Dan said, "I wanted to tell my

side of the stories, knowing well that there wasn't an iota of a chance for you to read them."

"So you felt sorry for Suzy, Mia, and now Amy?"

"Yes and no. It was a kind of yearning."

After a long minute, Lucy asked, "Wouldn't you confess now that all three girls in your books are, in fact, one and the same—Lucy Kim?"

Dan was quiet for a long time. "I never expected to meet you again, Lucy. My two books were already published, and the third was conceived long before this quirk of fate brought us together."

"It's a great revelation, after all these years. Just unbelievable." When Dan did not respond, she said, "Regardless, I should sue you."

When Dan seemed nonchalant, she stuck out her tongue at Dan, in an obvious anger. When Dan ignored her, she put her thumb in front of his eyes.

That triggered him to explode. "The stories tell you that I was in love with you. As I got older, the memories became sharper, and they were recurring every night until I put them down into the computer. It was PTSD. You were the prime source of my never-ending nightmares."

"Good for you, Dan. You deserve a whole lot more punishment. Can you imagine your own granddaughters kicking and screaming like me?"

"Oh no. Not them."

"You should go to hell."

They stayed one day in Santa Fe in the historic downtown that was busy with multiple festivals. When they arrived back at Dan's the next day, they stayed home doing nothing special, but Lucy enjoyed the hemp. She was now getting high from it. Dan gave her three jars of hemp ointment for her hip pain that he had bought earlier. At the end of the second day, Dan gathered his family at a restaurant. He was glad to see that his children were more relaxed, and his grandkids were very happy to see Lucy again.

Lucy said she hated to depart but she knew her own grandkids were waiting for her.

At the airport, she held Dan tight and said, "Colorado is a magnet to seniors also. I shall return."

In late July, when Lucy asked Dan to come to Chicago, Dan asked her to visit him instead, and she agreed. They made a short visit to Aspen and the nearby hot-springs resort. In mid-September they went camping in Monument Valley in northern Arizona. Lucy liked the John Wayne museum there.

EPILOGUE

One day in November, Dan received a shocking text message from Lucy's daughter Iris: "Mom has a massive brain hemorrhage from a ruptured aneurysm. She is on life support."

Dan called her right back. "What happened?" he asked.

"Mom had a severe, steady headache for several days, and she collapsed while I was visiting her."

Dan remembered that Lucy had complained of migraine headaches when she was in Denver, soon after their Yellowstone trip, and another time in Albuquerque. Dan knew he should have dragged her to ER, and it would haunt him for the rest of his life.

He flew to Chicago the next day. After arriving at a hotel near Lucy's hospital, Dan texted Iris: "If possible, could I visit her early in the morning?"

Iris called him right back. She said her brother would be at the hospital all night until six the next morning, and she'd be there at six. She said Dan could come in at five thirty, if that wasn't too early for him.

Dan took a taxi to the hospital. When he knocked on the ICU door, Peter came out looking tired but with a nice smile.

"How is she?" Dan asked.

"She is stable."

"How are the kids doing?"

"So far, so good, but time will tell," Peter said. He also said he didn't know Lucy had a brain aneurysm until now, and that Lucy's neurologist had urged all the family members to get a screening MRI, saying that it could be hereditary.

"I thought she was healthy," Dan said, "and I was going to go first." When Peter asked about his aneurysm, Dan said, "It's almost there. I need another echo next month, but I'm thinking of not taking surgery. It's because of my age."

That startled Peter, but he kept his emotion to himself. "My sister should be here in half an hour."

"Thank you, Dr. Peter."

They hugged for a long time. Soon Peter said, "Thank you very much for being so nice to our mom. She's been very happy for the past two years."

"No poker games?" said Dan to cheer him up.

"She quit gambling right after she met you, Dr. Dan," he said, in tears.

"Your mom was very nice to my grandkids."

Peter smiled at that before walking out of the ICU, still with tear-filled eyes.

When Dan was alone with Lucy, he kissed her cheek, carefully avoiding all the tubes and wires connected to her. Then he sat down next to her and held her hand: "We've been good friends and good companions, Lucy," he whispered. "And *semi-lovers*." He looked at Lucy, expecting her to smile. "Goodbye, Lucy." Then he whispered, "See you again in forty-five years, my dear Old Faithful."

He thanked Lucy for extending his life to a more lively and meaningful one. He did not have any regrets about Lucy or himself or to their deceased spouses or their families, especially their grandkids.

Exactly at six o'clock, Iris came in. Dan stood up, vacating the chair next to the bed.

"I thank you guys giving me a very private time with your mom."

"Not at all, Dr. Dan. We'll be pulling the plug out in three days, soon after our aunt comes from Korea."

"Aunt?" Dan asked in surprise.

"Yes, Mom's younger sister. Pulling the plug out was Mom's wish, rather than lingering forever, like our dad. We will have the funeral soon after. I'll let you know the details as soon as we arrange it."

"Thanks, Iris. But I won't be attending the funeral. Your mom told me not to."

"Oh? When did she tell you?"

"It was long time ago, but she said it would be okay to visit her grave. I've been to your dad's grave."

Iris turned away with her head down. When she turned back, her eyes were wet. They hugged for a minute without saying a word before Dan departed.

Two months later Dan received the printer's copy of his third book, *Near Miss*. That was the first printed book. His dedication in the book read, "To my wife, Linda, and my dear friend Lucy," and he planned to give it to Lucy.

A week later, he visited Lucy's tomb. After laying small bouquets of yellow roses on Lucy's and Charlie's graves, he placed the printer's copy of his book on Lucy's grave and thanked her for helping him to finish it. Dan realized his *semi-lover* was gone, but their miracle baby, *Near Miss*, would live forever.

After spending about an hour at the gravesite, he gathered all the flowers and book, and brought them back to the airport, as he did not want to leave any trace of him. In the airport he placed one rose in his carry-on bag before discarding the rest in the trash bin. After passing through the security, he pinned the rose in his breast pocket area.

Unlike his earlier idea of sending the printer's copy to Iris, Dan brought it back home. He did not want to disturb Lucy's family; he simply wanted to fade away, just like rainbows, without a trace. He was now nothing but Lucy's former companion and a former Facebook friend, both transient.

On the airplane Dan's thoughts went back to his discussions with Lucy on Sir Francis Bacon's essay: "Wives are young men's mistresses; companions for middle age; and old men's nurses."

Lucy had said the maxim needed an update even for the younger generation, and perhaps new essays on seniors—their plights in nursing, grieving, and falling in love. Dan thought semi-lovers also needed attention.

Like many other seniors, Lucy had lost her mate after putting up grueling nursing care for a long time. While still grieving, she fell in love with her old sweetheart, knowing well that he had only four years to live. Lucy tried to relish their relationship as much as possible, yet she kept it within her conscience to *semi-love*---an intimate companionship, their original puppy love.

Dan had met her again after seeing double rainbows, and now Lucy was gone, like rainbows. Dan remembered Lucy's saying that their senior romance was like rainbows—*precious but short and sweet.* Dan wondered if all the senior love was short and sweet like theirs—*like rainbows.*

APPENDIX

Author's Note: The original version of the following passage was published in my first book, *Wandering in the DMZ*, in 2016. Opinions expressed herein are solely my own.

History of Korea

"Whenever whales battle, it is a shrimp that
gets crushed," says a Korean proverb.
So even in peace, Korea catches a cold
if any of the leviathans sneezes.

Korean Peninsula

Present-day Korea is a peninsula in the Far East, about half the size of California. It directly shares northern borders with China and Russia. Japan is within a short sailing distance to the south. The United States has been in Korea since 1945, after World War II.

However, once upon a time, Koreans ruled a large portion of northeastern Asia, including present-day Manchuria and eastern Siberia, in addition to the peninsula. They were vigorous people and occasionally made incursions into mainland China. A series of Chinese empires built the Great Wall to ward them off.

Kokuryo (고구려, 高句麗) was one of the dominating Korean kingdoms for a long time, but gradually it was pushed into the peninsula. Koryeo (고려, 高麗) followed it, which became known to the West as Korea. The Yi dynasty succeeded it in the fourteenth century. It was a hermit kingdom, also known as Joseon (조선, 朝鮮, Morning Calm).

Koreans are the eighth-largest minority of China's two billion people, most of them living in northern China. Some areas are officially bilingual, including Yanbian Korean Autonomous Prefecture.

There are three Korean subgroups in China and also in Eastern Siberia: *Koryo-jok (고려족)* are natives, direct descendants of ancient Korean kingdoms; *Josun-jok* (조선족) are descendants of refugees from the Japanese-occupied peninsula at the turn of the twentieth century. The third subgroup is the latest refugees from starving North Korea. China routinely arrests and sends them back, so they have melted into the population as illegals.

During the World War II, Josef Stalin forcibly relocated Siberian Koreans into the Soviet inland because they looked like Japanese. That was when the United States interned Hawaiian Japanese in concentration camps in the western United States.

Koreans in Russia and the former USSR are called *Koryo Saram*, meaning the same as *Koryo Jok* in Manchuria. After being pushed around for several generations, some of them became prominent, among them, *Roman Kim* is a virtuoso violinist from Kazakhstan.

Some Korean descendants elsewhere also became famous. Among them is seventeen-year-old Chloe Kim from California, who won a gold medal for the United States in snowboarding in the 2018 Winter Olympics in Pyeongchang, South Korea, her parents' homeland.

Geopolitical Crossroads

Genghis Khan came down to Korea and then tried to invade Japan. Samurais assaulted Korean shores from time to time. Imperial Japan annexed Korea in 1906. They soon occupied Manchuria and marched down mainland China and then on to Burma. They also invaded the Philippines and attacked Pearl Harbor.

In 1945, at the end of World War II, Imperial Japan handed Korea over to the United States, but the US asked the USSR to disarm remnants of the Imperial Japanese Army north of the thirty-eighth parallel. The USSR stayed on, thus dividing the Korean peninsula into two.

They installed Kim Il-Sung in North Korea, while the United States brought in Dr. Syngman Rhee, a PhD from Princeton University, to head South Korea.

On June 25, 1950, North Korea invaded South Korea. The United States came to help South Korea, along with a sixteen-nation United Nations force. Then China entered the war to rescue North Korea, resulting in a direct land war between the Communist China and the United States. The Korean War, simply known as 6/25 to Koreans, ended in a cease-fire in 1953 along the demilitarized zone (DMZ).

The Korean War left behind a huge human toll: in addition to a near million military casualties on both sides, untold number of civilians were killed, maimed, abducted, and separated from families. Also more than a million North Koreans sought safe haven in South Korea, many of them walking down through bitterly cold winter storms---a major human migration in modern history.

Cultural Crossroads

Korea was a cultural crossroads as well. Buddhism and earlier Chinese cultures arrived on the peninsula and then passed on to Japan. Located at the eastern end of the Silk Road, the peninsula saw the arrival of Western cultures, including Christianity, which also passed on to Japan. During the Japanese occupation from 1906 to 1945, Imperial Japan applied brutal assimilation policies.

During the Korean War of 1950–1953, more than one million foreign troops from all over the world were stationed in Korea, bringing diverse cultures with them.

Religions in Korea

Buddhism dominated Korea until the fourteenth century, when the founding emperor of the Yi Dynasty kicked them out of population centers for corruption, replacing it with Confucianism. They even called it Yoo-Gyo (유교), similar to Bool-Gyo (불교) for Buddhism.

During their occupation from 1905 to 1945, Imperial Japan forcibly imposed Shintoism on Koreans, with their emperor as a living god.

The first wave of Christianity arrived in Korea several centuries earlier via the Silk Road. The second wave was missionaries wading up the southern shores in the eighteenth century. Both were gentle missionaries, while the third wave came with a big bang of the Korean War of 1950–1953, shadowing millions of Western troops.

Although Christianity dominates Korea, with one-third of its population, and Buddhism has resurged, more than half of Koreans still do not have a religious affiliation, they say.

Korean Ethics (1945–1964)

Boys and girls could not hold their hands in public. They were not allowed to dance, so there were no proms in high schools. Kissing in public was viewed as lewd. Adulterers were paraded in public, handcuffed, and received a long jail time.

The South Korean government censored Western movies and books and banned anything Japanese. They arrested anyone who possessed any materials related to Communism. The National Police were busy as morality and culture police, with spies everywhere.

ABOUT THE AUTHOR

Kenneth K. Suh lives in the Midwest with his wife.

Printed in the United States
By Bookmasters